The piano teacher watched Barbara carefully as she came nearer. The clock on the mantelpiece read three-ten, so they'd have to hurry. In fifteen minutes Amanda would be home on the bus. He held his hand out and motioned for Barbara to sit next to him.

"I have to tell you something, Harmon," she began. "It can't go on like last week. That was too painful."

"I know, sweetheart," he said. "Your problem is that you let yourself get carried away. That's always dangerous. Moderation . . . that's the name of the game."

"It's too hard for me sometimes. I can never get you at home, and you don't like me leaving those messages with your service. You only come here on Tuesdays . . ."

He shrugged. "Be happy I come here at all."

She gave him a black look. "If Leo knew he'd kill me."

"Well, that's a lot better than if he took it into his head to kill me," the piano teacher said. "I hate violence. It's so . . . artless."

Also by Richard Barth
Published by Fawcett Books:

BLOOD DOESN'T TELL
DEADLY CLIMATE
THE CONDO KILL
ONE DOLLAR DEATH
A RAGGED PLOT
THE RAG BAG CLAN

FURNISHED FOR MURDER

Richard Barth

FAWCETT CREST • NEW YORK

A Fawcett Crest Book
Published by Ballantine Books
Copyright © 1991 by Richard Barth

Library of Congress Catalog Card Number: 90-37260

ISBN 0-449-22083-4

This edition published by arrangement with St. Martin's Press, Inc.

Manufactured in the United States of America

First Ballantine Books Edition: March 1993

This book is dedicated with love to my sister, Ellen Geltzer, and my sister-in-law, Ronni Kleinman, two very brave women.

One

LEO PERKINS HEARD THE SOFT FLUTTER OF wings before he actually saw the first greenhead flying low over the cornfield. The bird braked in that semicomical way of leaning against the direction of flight and laid out its webbed landing gear in front of it. The water of the little pond at the edge of the cornfield rippled with the impact and then subsided. The duck looked around, apparently was pleased at its choice of location, then darted its head under the water for its lunch.

Leo was chilled to the bone and wondering what in hell a forty-five-year-old suburbanite was doing out on some farmer's back sixty acres rather than in his own heated living room watching the Giants. Early November was for analyzing the success of earlier draft choices and midseason position realignments, not for discussions on the correct load of ten-gauge No. 2s for the three-and-a-half-inch shotgun shells. Besides, ballistics was an issue Leo had no ideas about, this being his first time hunting ducks. Full choke, partial choke . . . who knew? He did what he was instructed to do by his friend Sollie and lay down on the frosted earth and waited quietly. For a man six foot three inches, two hundred and five pounds big, lying quietly was not easy. Between the dozen little stones pushing against his body and the broken corn stubble impaling him, Leo was uncomfortable. So much for the joys of camaraderie, he thought.

The two men were lying in the stubble of the cornfield five yards away from the edge of the pond. Sollie's quivering dog,

Bonaparte, was between them. Leo nudged Sollie with his toe and indicated the mallard, the first of the morning.

Sollie motioned with his hand to wait. Leo had no idea what for. His fingers were freezing and the sooner he got his duck and got back in the car, the better. There had to be a place to get coffee nearby. Forty-five minutes lying prone on the cold ground was about his limit.

The orange-legged Canadian greenhead bobbing in the water was a big duck, fully plumed and with a layer of fat that was supposed to make eating it a delight, but Leo supposed the appearance of one bird meant more were on their way. He grimaced and tried to shift into a more comfortable position. Sollie frowned at him and put a finger up to his lips. Damn, Leo thought, working his frozen fingers back and forth to get the blood flowing. Capiletti's Meat Market in Harrison would have been easier.

The two men raised their heads slightly at the sound of a distant whir of wings. Within eight minutes another half dozen birds had landed, and the small pond began to look like a carnival target booth. Still Sollie waited. He knew the promise of floating scrap corn kernels and the security of brother mallards would bring in another dozen birds. The problem was with Bonaparte. The Brittany spaniel by their side was more accustomed to suburban Westchester than the fields of Schoharie County, and there was no telling how long he could contain his baser instinct to pounce. After five more of the big curly-tailed birds landed on the pond, Sollie started to crawl into a better firing position. The birds were unaware of the two men so close by in the corn stubble. Ten seconds maybe, and Sollie would give the signal.

But suddenly, through the deathly silence, the sharp noise of a watch alarm intruded, and the dozen birds shot up as though the surface of the pond had suddenly turned into a skillet. Sollie cursed and took five precious seconds to stand up and get into position with his shotgun to his shoulder. Leo jumped up also and started yanking the trigger.

''God damn that alarm,'' Sollie cursed, and tried to hit a duck that was ten yards farther away than it should have been. He missed, missed with the second barrel, and bent quickly to reload. Leo fired at one farther away. He watched in surprise as it stopped flapping its wings as though its battery had been turned off and tumbled headfirst back into the pond. His second shot went wide of a bird that had made it past the treetops. Two more shots rang out from Leo's left, and Sollie shouted delightedly as one of them found a bird that was forty yards away. They both reloaded, but by the time they brought their guns up again, the sky around them was empty. The Brittany spaniel, being more of a flusher than a retriever, hesitated to go into the cold water for the first duck, but Sollie urged him on. The drake floated, an oily rag in a foam of feathers. In a minute it was lying at Sollie's feet and Bonaparte was shaking himself off. Then the dog took off for the bird slapped out of the sky by Sollie's load of heavy, half-choked shot. The smell of cordite lingered over the field as the dog came back. After dropping the second bird next to the first, he stood waiting for the praise he knew he was due. His owner patted him once, then turned around and went over to Leo with a look that was not meant to ingratiate. "What the hell was that noise?" he growled.

Leo looked sheepish. "My watch. Little alarm goes off every hour."

Sollie shook his head as he looked down at the two birds. "Could have had us a half dozen easy," he said. "Next time turn the goddamn thing off."

Leo nodded but thought sure as hell there wasn't going to be a next time. The sight of the little bird sagging out of the sky bit his memory.

Two

THE RIVETZ FURNITURE STORE WHERE LEO and Sollie were employed was located off Mamaroneck Avenue in White Plains. It encompassed more than fifty thousand square feet of display area with an additional one hundred thousand square feet of warehouse facility. Inside this vast arena was just about every conceivable article of furniture, every current swatch of fabric or leather to upholster these items in, enough chrome and glass to re-create the New York Pavilion at the '64 World's Fair, and enough wood to provide paper for a week's worth of *National Enquirer*s. This was a furniture supermarket, the embodiment of a marketing concept to rival Henry Ford's revolutionary notions about manufacturing. While there were acres of merchandise in styles ranging from pre–Greco/Roman to postmodern, the heaviest concentration had an Italian influence. Turning a Westchester house into something resembling an eighteenth-century Tuscan loggia would have been a piece of cake for the professionals at the store. "Rivetz Has It" was the motto emblazoned above the entire complex and repeated a mind-searing fifty times a day on local TV and radio stations. And if, by chance, Rivetz didn't have it on the floor, then there was always the warehouse, which was, in the words of their best publicist, a vast playground for the discriminating buyer.

This "playground" was in a building the size of three football fields and seventy feet tall, set on a concrete pad with industrial steel shelves reaching from floor to ceiling. These shelves were broken into compartments, each capable of containing a small car, but instead holding a couch, or a dining table, or a Barcalounger, or some other article of furniture. Row upon row of varnished or upholstered items trapped in large cages. The Alcatraz of furniture stores. And moving up and down these aisles were heavy-duty forklift trucks to reach up the fifty or so feet and pluck down the three-cushion, pleated-skirt, sloped-back sleeper sofa with the burgundy flame-stitch pattern . . . just like the lady ordered. An observer felt like an ant in a doll house. The Rivetz salesmen knew their merchandise and sold it with a passion befitting men on a 5 percent draw—all, that is, except Leo Perkins, who had found that whatever he did, he still took home the same five hundred and change a week. The way he figured it, people were going to buy when they were ready, and there was not much a salesman could do to convince someone that what she really needed was a whole new dining-room set if she just came in for a replacement chair. No way in hell, so he just waited at the order desk and responded politely when a customer asked for assistance.

Leo Perkins was in Dining Rooms and happy to be there. It gave you a chance to get some reading done, unlike Bedding where Sollie worked, or Lighting where Hanley was. Those places were always jumping. From any sales analysis, you'd think all people did was wear out their mattresses screwing and then turn around and throw lamps at each other. Anyway, one large dining-room ensemble added up to a gross of wall sconces. Not that he hadn't tried other things . . . like last year's flirtation with Children's Furniture. But one week was all he could take, the way those women came in with specifications for their kids' desks. They called them "work stations"; you'd think each one was harboring a little Einstein.

Orantes came up to Leo and motioned to his watch. The little sonofabitch, Leo thought. Exercising the rights of his office like some goddamn little colonel. Orantes was section head over Dining Rooms, Lighting, and Carpets. His job was to monitor sales, give pep talks, rearrange the displays, set the holiday schedules, but more important, tell his people when to go to lunch. For this he got a guaranteed forty grand a year, and he didn't have to sell so much as a prayer rug. A college grad, no less. Four years, so he can tell me when it's twelve-thirty.

Leo put on his jacket, slipped the brown bag with his tuna-fish sandwich out of the drawer where he was sitting, and headed toward the little room set out back for employee lunches. What with all the millions of dollars worth of furniture out front, it was a cruel joke that the decor of the lunchroom was strictly linoleum and cracked vinyl. But Leo liked the lunchroom, since he had forty-five minutes to talk with his friends and maybe even get in a quick game of chess.

Hanley grinned at him as he entered. The two men had a shared distaste for Orantes and both owned houses in Harrison. Paul Hanley was short, with a lean jogger's body, thinning red hair, and a face that had enough lines on it to make him look ten years older than his forty-two. Leo was much taller at six foot three and also prided himself on staying in shape by using a home rowing machine that Barbara had bought for his last birthday. A boat on the Sound would have been better, but how could you beat $95.98 including instruction manual?

Hanley pointed to the seat next to him. "Care to dine with me?"

"If you don't mind sitting down with a guy who hasn't had a sale all morning," Leo said. "I might get nasty." He slumped next to his friend and withdrew the sandwich. He looked at it for a moment without moving. "Sollie tell you about the hunt?" he asked.

"Yeah. He didn't know whether to laugh or cry. I think that's the last invitation you'll get." Hanley took a bite of his own sandwich. "Well, I think you still got an open invitation at the poker game. We're on this Friday."

Leo shook his head. "You know that's not my game."

"I don't know why you got to go to that dump, McArdle's, every Friday night," Hanley said. "We could use an extra hand."

"Get Orantes," Leo said with a smile.

"Fuck Orantes, that asshole ain't getting inside my door. You know what he did to Collins last week? Made him stay late dusting the tops of the track lights. Now, who the fuck looks up on the top of the track lights?" Hanley leaned back. "The guy's a real jerk."

"You want coffee?" Leo asked.

"Yeah, light and sweet. That machine doesn't know from regular." He flipped fifty cents onto the table and Leo took it on his way to the back of the room. When he came back Hanley had the paper open and was looking through the sports section. Sollie spotted the two of them as he walked in and came over.

"You believe those Jets . . . those idiots," Sollie said. "Two screen passes for interceptions . . . against the Bills no less." He rolled his eyes. "It's a good thing we weren't near a TV yesterday. I would have died."

"I think I'm going back to watching college ball," Hanley said. "I can't wait until baseball season."

"What, so the Mets can break your heart again?" Leo said.

"Hey, you're forgetting '86."

"They just did that to set you guys up for seven more years of anguish. Stick with the Yankees . . . no illusions." Leo took a sip of his coffee and made a face. "That machine doesn't know from coffee, period."

"So," Sollie asked, "any sales this morning?"

Leo shook his head. "It's been quiet."

"Wait 'til you hear this one." Sollie leaned forward and his face took on an impish grin.

"Mrs. Williams comes in from Scarsdale, gotta be eighty if she's a day . . . Very proper, very grandmotherly . . . nice clothes. The guy she's with is under his own steam, but just barely, he's got a cane and sits down on every flat surface he can find. So she asks about the special on the Sealy Posturepedic XP50 that we've been running in all the papers. You know, two twins for the price of one on that load of mattresses in the warehouse we overbought. Mrs. Williams wants to know if she can get the Sealy King, the XY10, for half-price also. I explain the deal to her and she just shakes her head. 'I need a king,' she says. So how about you buy the two twins and put them together, I tell her. Same size. Remember now she's gotta be over eighty. She leans closer and lowers her voice. 'I wouldn't want Herman worrying about getting caught in the crack coming over,' she says.'' Sollie leaned back. "Now how do you like that?''

The two other men applauded.

"How old you figure Herman is?'' Paul asked.

"Ninety easy,'' Sollie said. "He should be giving seminars.''

"Christ, why didn't I marry a Mrs. Williams,'' Hanley said and shook his head. "Seems like all the active women are under twenty-five or over seventy-five.''

"So wait five years,'' Leo added. "Herman can't last too much longer and then she'll be available.''

"Thanks,'' Hanley said and slapped the newspaper open.

"Don't take it personally,'' Sollie said. "I don't suppose any of us got a Mrs. Williams at home.'' He looked over at Leo and smirked. "Or what?''

Leo looked him square in the face and said with mock dignity, "There are other things in life equally as important as good sex. Good sandwiches, for instance.'' Their explosion of laughter made some of the men at the surrounding tables look over at them. Hanley took another bite of his food and went back to his paper. After a minute he shook his head.

"Christ, every day I thank the Lord I moved out of Queens. Here's a story about a high-school science teacher in Astoria that was busted for abusing one of the kids in his lab.''

"Showing her some new jean-splitting experiment, I suppose,'' Sollie said with a grin.

"What, it's a garden of Eden up here in Westchester?'' Leo asked. "What about all the drugs in the high schools?''

"It's all the black kids,'' Hanley offered.

"Don't fool yourself,'' Leo said. "There's more drugs in the Scarsdale high-school parking lot than at Pathmark. Amanda's only twelve and she knows what's going on, and that's in Harrison, not Scarsdale. Harrison kids' allowances don't rival the GNP of a small African nation.''

"At least it's clean everywhere,'' Sollie said. "You been to the city lately?''

"With the taxes I pay on my crummy split level they could

sponge and talcum the streets of Harrison every night, for Chrissake." Leo took a swallow of his coffee and sat back.

"Don't mind Leo," Hanley said. "He's in one of his knock Westchester moods." He motioned to his temple. "Happens every time there's a full moon."

"Which is hard enough to see through all the pollution," Leo said. "What kind of a place is this?"

"The kind of place you can get all sorts of private lessons for your kids. Sarah's jealous of all the things the other kids are doing," Hanley said. "She even mentioned your Amanda and her piano lessons. I get it twice a night, coming and going."

Leo shook his head. "If I had my way I'd rather see Amanda concentrate more on her homework. But Barbara thinks that other stuff makes her more 'well rounded,' whatever that means."

"As far as I can tell, 'well rounded' means a kid with a father who's into a second mortgage," Hanley said. "Or am I wrong?"

Leo smiled. "Something like that. Seriously though, you never thought of Florida . . . maybe Texas? If only to get away from Orantes. There's a Rivetz in Tampa and one in Fort Pierce."

"You're kidding," Sollie said. "Where'd I go hunting?"

"Crocodiles," Leo said. "Or maybe you'd take up fishing."

Sollie laughed. "Can you see the look on Bonaparte's face when he dives into the water and comes up with a 'gator?" He took a bite of his sandwich and shook his head. "Maybe you're young enough to change, but not me, not my dog, and certainly not my Alice."

"Yeah, it's always the wives," Leo said disgustedly. "But that doesn't mean you gotta stop trying."

"In your case," Hanley said, "I think it does."

Three

BARBARA PERKINS WAS FIDDLING WITH the begonias when the doorbell rang. She looked at her watch, made a mental note that Harmon Parrish was right on schedule again, and headed for the front door. He had arrived that afternoon dressed once again in his soft Missoni sweater and Armani double-pleated pants. Harmon Parrish, the well-known pianist, winner of numerous local and statewide competitions, the 1968 Bogardus Fellow in European music, and a fixture in Westchester recital halls for more than two decades, had arrived for his afternoon lesson with Amanda. Barbara stood aside to let him in.

At fifty-two, Parrish moved with the light step of a much younger man. He was of average height, with a physique that hadn't changed in years. His face seemed unlined and the only giveaway of his age was the shock of white hair that outshone Toscanini's. His were the kind of looks that made other men uneasy; that hair, symbol of old age, set upon a vibrant, almost youthful, face. It was unsettling. But the women loved it. It gave him presence, ratified his status as a musician and an "artist," and made him different from their workaday husbands with their buttoned-down, pinstripe wardrobes. Harmon brought an air of sophistication to the houses where he taught. There certainly were other piano teachers in Westchester, middle-aged women and younger musicians still working on their curriculum vitaes, but few had as busy a schedule or charged quite as much. But then he was Harmon Parrish, and the thirty-five dollars bought not only his incomparable skills for forty-five minutes, but also snob appeal. Most of Harmon's students were the little rich kids of Westchester and lower Connecticut, the ones whose parents lived in large houses with sloping manicured lawns. If Harmon Parrish wasn't the best, he certainly worked hard at giving that impression. Getting his Tuesday three-thirty time slot had been Barbara's biggest coup of 1989 and one she guarded zealously through all the arguments with Leo about the incredible expense. Harmon had explained that he usually didn't teach in Harrison but that in fact it was on a direct route between an earlier appointment in Larchmont and one in Greenwich. "Aren't you lucky," he had announced at their first meeting over half a year ago. And he was being modest.

The piano teacher moved without hesitation into the living room and sat down on the sofa. He watched Barbara carefully as she came nearer. The clock on the mantelpiece read three-ten, so they'd have to hurry. In fifteen minutes Amanda would be home on the bus. He held his hand out and motioned for Barbara to sit next to him. She rubbed her hands to get off the vermiculite from the begonias, then sat down.

"I have to tell you something, Harmon," she began. "It can't go on like last week. That was too painful."

"I know, sweetheart," he said. "Your problem is that you let yourself get carried away. That's always dangerous. Moderation . . . that's the name of the game."

"It's too hard for me sometimes. I can never get you at home, and you don't like me leaving those messages with your service. You only come here on Tuesdays . . ."

He shrugged. "Be happy I come here at all."

She gave him a black look.

"After all, before I came into your life you were bored silly in this little excuse of a house. What other excitement did you have?" He chuckled.

"Don't be nasty."

"I'm being realistic, sugar. Now both you and Amanda look forward to Tuesdays. What could be better?"

"I'm not so sure about Amanda."

"Yes, well, she's having trouble with the Mendelssohn."

He looked at his watch. "She'll be home in ten minutes, we'd better hurry." He bent over and reached into his briefcase, which contained the sheet music for his lessons. He pulled out a small envelope, removed the note from inside, and scanned it for a moment. "So now you're sending me letters?"

"Sometimes it's the only way I have to contact you."

He put the note back in casually with the music. "So you're willing to take a big risk this time." He smiled coyly. "How big?"

Barbara leaned over toward him. As she did she pulled out a fat envelope from a side pocket. "This much," she said.

"Good." Harmon Parrish smiled.

"If Leo knew he'd kill me." She hesitated only a second before handing it to him.

"Well, that's a lot better than if he took it into his head to kill me," the piano teacher said and slipped the envelope into the pocket of his Armani pants. "I hate violence. It's so . . . artless."

"No, No, NO! This section is *diminuendo*." Harmon threw his hand to his forehead. "It's not supposed to sound like a herd of elephants cavorting on the keyboard. Mendelssohn is subtle, Amanda, subtle. Here . . ." Parrish played the section softly. "Hark! The Herald Angels Sing" never sounded so romantic to Amanda's twelve-year-old ears before but she figured, if that's the way he wants it, that's the way he'll get it. She played the piece again, trying to lighten her touch on the keyboard. Christmas was still two months away, but she wanted to have at least two songs to perform before the junior high school assembly. After all, one year's worth of lessons should have more to show for it than "The Peanut Vendor" and "The Song of the Toad."

"Quarter note, then the half . . . slide them together, 'Peace on earth, and mercy mild' . . . like that. My dear, you're not trying."

Amanda felt like crying. Of course she was trying, but how could she do anything with him carping away like that? What a twit, she thought.

"Dum dum dum, softly, softly, da dum dum dummmm. That's it.'' He looked at his watch. "Ten of four. Time for your independent summary.'' He got up from the bench and stretched his arms behind him. Without hesitating he turned and walked out of the living room.

Thank God, Amanda thought. Seven minutes of peace. She played the section from the Mendelssohn carol over three times and then summarized the other small piece of music she had been learning. This was the best time for her. "Independent summary'' was part of Parrish's teaching method, a seven-minute block when he left her alone to practice in private all that he had shown her during the lesson. This was supposed to bring out self-reliance and the ability to fine-tune oneself before a performance. When the independent summary was over Amanda knew she was going to have to play the two pieces for him flawlessly, but at least for seven minutes she wouldn't have him breathing down her neck and making twitty comments. Piano lessons . . . ugh, who needed them? She kept hoping that her father would win in the argument with her mother, but deep down in her heart she knew that it was hopeless. The only argument she ever saw her mother lose was with the usher at a Broadway play when it was discovered they had tickets for a week later. Well, it was a tradeoff. She liked the special attention at assemblies, so she just had to put up with Mr. Parrish and his sickly sweet after-shave lotion and his supercilious manners. Now there was a wonderful word. She was so glad she had learned it the week before. Super-silly-us Mr. Parrish. She tried the Mendelssohn piece once more just as he returned.

"Now Amanda. Concert performance time,'' he said and sat down in one of the armchairs in the living room. "Impress me.''

"Now Constance. Concert performance time,'' he said and sat down in the Sapporiti cream-colored leather lounger. "Impress me.'' It was an hour later and Parrish was finishing up his Larchmont lesson with twelve-year-old Constance Eberhard. They were in the Eberhards' music room, one of the more than fifteen rooms in the large, plantation-style estate. Mr. Eberhard, who had put this glorious life-style together, including the three full-time servants and a score of Impressionist and Renaissance paintings to soften the bold lines of the signature modern furniture, was not at home. He was only at home between the hours of eight in the evening and seven in the morning, at which latter time he was whisked away from the slumbering mansion by his chauffeur to travel once again to the city. Parrish understood that he did something with bonds, but what exactly or for whom was unclear. What was clear was that neither Mr. nor Mrs. Eberhard had the slightest interest in Constance's musical progress. But with the three servants tooting around, there was never a shortage of hands to open the door for Parrish when he rang, even if the Mr. and Mrs. were away on one of their trips.

The smell of money in the Eberhards' household was inescapable. Every surface had been labored over with great concern by some artisan, whether it was the hand-stitched leather of the furniture, the rubbed-wood joinery of the marquetry floor, or the intimate painting on the detailed finger molding. Everything was spotless, even the inside of the Steinway grand piano, which was vacuumed, Parrish was assured by the maid Theresa, once a day. Unfortunately, this didn't help Constance's playing at all. From out of the glistening Steinway came a noise that sounded more like the inside of a recycling plant than Beethoven's music.

The young girl hesitated four times in the first section of the minuet in G major. Parrish glanced out the alarm-wired window, past the two-acre back lawn to the bulkheading and the harbor beyond. The notes from the piano came at him in a seemingly random pattern bearing little relationship to the music as written, and Parrish wished he were somewhere else, maybe on the Eberhard sailboat bobbing at the dock, maybe back at the Perkinses', where at least Amanda could string a few notes together. But this was painful. Parrish held up his hand.

"Thank you, Constance. I think we have to stop for the day." He rose and patted the young girl on the shoulder.

"The left hand needs a lot more work. Next week I want the Beethoven to be perfect."

Constance walked with her teacher to the front door. Theresa was in the hall, dusting the molding on the walnut paneling, and as Harmon Parrish passed, she smiled at him. It was, as far as smiles go, beyond the offhanded polite farewell, and something a bit closer to a leer. But it was lost on Parrish, who had his eyes only on the front door and his reprieve. "See you next week," he called after him as he closed the door, and Theresa stopped her dusting for a moment.

"Mr. Harmon's a hard teacher, ain't he now?" the maid said as Constance turned to go to her room upstairs. "Very serious, he seems."

"I don't know," Constance said and started climbing the curving staircase. "Sometimes I think he isn't paying much attention. You know what I mean?"

The young maid shook her head and the little white collar on her black uniform jiggled up and down. "No, I wouldn't know," she said. "He never talks to me."

Harmon's five o'clock lesson on Tuesday was with Adrian Wick, only a few miles away in Belle Haven. Somewhere in Adrian's ancestry there was probably a Wickenham, or Wickford, or possibly even a Wicksley, so laden was his house with old English antiques. Family heirlooms, Parrish figured. But the house was not as large as the Eberhards'. This was old money. How else could Harmon explain the fancy address? Mr. Wick was an associate professor at Columbia—German history or something. Surely it couldn't be accounted for by a contribution from Mrs. Wick, who was studying for her real estate license after finally getting the last of her children into first grade the year before.

Teaching at the Wickses' was relatively painless for Parrish. Unlike his other students, fourteen-year-old Adrian had some real talent and took direction beautifully. He had mastered the Fletcher beginning piano books within two months, worked easily through the more simple Bach two-part inventions, and was now on the longer, more difficult

Mozard C Major Sonata. He approached the work with the same kind of dedication Parrish thought he had noted in the father, the same thoroughness. One day when Adrian was into his "independent summary," Harmon had wandered into the library of the house. Two things struck him: There were more books on eighteenth-century German history than he could have imagined ever being published, and the books were alphabetically arranged. Very methodical—same as the kid.

Actually, Adrian wasn't such a kid. At fourteen he was strong enough to loosen piano strings with the force of his playing. Harmon had mentioned that to him early on, explaining that tuning pianos was costly and breaking pins was even worse. Since then Adrian had tried to play a little more *pianissimo*.

"There are no breaks between the triplets," Harmon said forcefully. "And you're leaving out notes right and left. You trying to be the composer?"

"I think it sounds nicer my way," Adrian said in mock defense.

"I suppose that's intended to be funny. Don't look at your fingerings, look at the notes."

Adrian played another small section while Harmon leaned back and watched.

"Hold it," he jumped in. "What's this note?" he asked pointing at the music.

"D," the boy said tentatively.

"You're fourteen years old and you need glasses? It's not a D. The third line—a B. And make it sound like a B, not like an F with a hernia."

"Yes sir," Adrian said and started the section over. This time he played it flawlessly. When he was finished, he looked over to his teacher for instruction.

"Well, go on," Parrish commented. "The piece doesn't end there." And so they continued until "independent summary" time, when Harmon took himself out of the room and let the boy put the finishing touches on one final run-through. On Tuesdays Adrian's mother took his little brother to an after-school karate class and Adrian's father had his evening class in the city, so the two of them were alone with the housekeeper. Parrish stayed out of the room for several minutes, wandering slowly through the rest of the downstairs. From the living room came the sounds of young Adrian diligently trying to work the ending just so. When Parrish reentered he smiled benignly at his pupil. "Okay, concert time, Adrian. Impress me."

Four

THERE WERE ONLY TWO CHESS CLUBS IN all of Westchester, and McArdle's was decidedly the cheaper spread. It was set upstairs in what once had been the refinishing studio of an antique shop, which accounted for the faint bouquet of varnish wafting through the room. The space was large enough for six tables, one soft-drink machine (which was almost always disabled), a hot plate with a battered tea kettle and some chipped mugs, a steel desk that had last seen duty in a National Guard armory, and an assortment of straight-back and upholstered chairs from every flea market north of Yonkers. Fortunately for the players, furniture refinishing needed good lighting, which accounted for the six large fluorescent fixtures bathing the club in enough light to blind an Arctic explorer. In an effort to keep the noise level down, one of the members had donated a carpet, which now had enough cigarette burns in it to play connect-the-dots with an entire kindergarten class. The walls held every unwanted painting from the club's seventy-odd members including a most romantic vase of paint-by-numbers flowers. One would have thought that this shabby second-story environment could not compete with home and hearth, but then chess players, given the nature of their obsession, would be happy to convene in a rest room as long as there was a board and thirty-two pieces.

Leo Perkins loved McArdle's. He loved the fact that on a given night he could walk in and sit down to a game of chess and keep the rest of his life as distant as the traffic flowing noisily past the small building. He loved the sense of balance and expectation as he opened on a fresh game and the feeling of victory and reaffirmation when he manipulated himself into a mating position. Even in losing there was only the briefest moment of despair, then an immediate high of hope for the possibilities of the next game. There was nothing like it, not sex, not fine food, not the quiet enjoyment of a good book, and certainly nothing the three networks could offer . . . nothing compared with the wily campaigns that took place on the sixty-four squares of a chessboard. In that small space existed a world of adventure so diverse that no computer game invented could compare with it.

Leo Perkins understood that, as did the other members of the club. Every night they came, dressed in elegant three-piece business suits or torn blue jeans and T-shirts with names of local auto parts stores. Moguls played with mongrels, and the great leveler was the board between them and their thirty-two pieces. Leo played with them all, but the person he enjoyed struggling against most was Jakob Barzeny.

Barzeny was something of a celebrity at the club. He lived on the generosity of friends and the odd dollars he could hustle by giving lessons. No one knew where he slept between midnight and 10:00 A.M. when the club was closed. But by ten-thirty he would be upstairs with a steaming glass of tea in front of him and a broad grin on his wizened face to greet the first members to appear. Barzeny was a Russian emigré and rumor had it that he had once been in the Russian Chess Academy, had drawn a game with Tal, and could beat anything or anyone New York placed in front of him. He had appeared at the club sometime in 1987 and had been a fixture there ever since. His English was adequate, his sense of humor heroic. He could always be counted on to have an observation about everyone and never hesitated sharing these opinions with whoever was nearby. He had good-naturedly insulted just about everyone in the club, and still they brought him sandwiches and cups of soup and cakes to eat. There was always the concern that one day he would just disappear as he had appeared, and so perhaps the food was a way of bribing him to remain.

Barzeny had two basic outfits. One was a suit the color of rust that had originally been made for a man two sizes larger. He wore this in the winter with a selection of thrift-shop shirts. The other included a dark-gray pair of polyester slacks, so shiny on the seat and knees they looked waterproof. Regardless of the temperature, he wore this with a navy cardigan sweater that at one time might have had a discernible pattern to the stitching but was now nothing but color, yarn, and little pills. Sometimes he wore a raincoat whose pockets showed their exhaustion, and he always wore his hat. It was the kind of dark cap that Israeli taxi drivers wear in Manhattan, and it was so much a part of him that no one in the club could ever recall seeing his bare head. His hair stuck out from under the sides in some disarray, but his lined face looked anything but confused. His eyes were dark green, the color of deep sea kelp, and once they held you, they never gave up their grip. His forehead was as broad as a Siberian peasant's but his chin was beardless small and pointed. One only had to imagine an older, beardless Lenin with a taxi cap on and there was Barzeny. He was, he claimed, sixty-two, but maybe that was counting by the Russian calendar. He once described a game he had witnessed between Botvinnik and Capablanca that took place in 1936—a time when he would have been eight years old. But no one pressed him on his age; they were too busy trying to outwit his sweeping offenses and uncanny defenses. While he played with everyone, even the patzers and hacks who lasted no more than a few minutes, no one beat him, not even Tontini, a local visiting grandmaster. Those who came close remembered their game long afterward.

Leo was no patzer. While he was uninterested in state or national rankings, he knew where he stood in relation to the

other members of the club. There were only two he couldn't
beat—Barzeny and Segroy, who was the club's director. The
trouble with playing with Segroy was that he was always
being interrupted to answer the phone or to adjudicate some
dispute at another table or even to handle some petty request
like making change for the soft-drink machine when it was
working or to let the repairman in when it wasn't. All of this
was very disturbing if one was playing by the clock, which
one did at McArdle's. Leo preferred to test himself against
Barzeny, which meant that Leo always arrived at the club
with a cup of chicken soup from Griben's Delicatessen. God
forbid it should be from the nearby diner instead. Besides
being a chess master, Barzeny knew his soups. In his haste
to get to the club this evening, however, Leo had presented
Barzeny with a container of diner split pea soup and was now
suffering the consequences.

"This is soup?" Barzeny grumbled and pushed his bishop
into a discovered queen pin. "They make better soup in Russian jails."

"And how would you know about that, Comrade Jakob?"
Leo asked.

"I know," Barzeny said, "because I know . . . don't ask.
There." He pointed. "You make me angry with this dish-
water and now I take revenge on your innocent little queen."

"She's not dead yet," Leo said, studying the board.

"Bukharin had better chance of escaping in '38. Your
move."

Leo, conceding his queen, tried to mount an attack on
Barzeny's king. He moved his rook down the board and said
"check."

"So, I distracted you with queen pin. Your check should
come two moves later. Now you have left knight unpro-
tected. Patience, Leo, in chess and in life, is big virtue."
Barzeny moved his king out of check toward the knight, and
Leo found himself in a spread-eagle position about to have
both legs chopped off. He looked on the shambles of his
strategy and offered his hand. "I promise next time the soup
will come from Griben's. Maybe you won't be so rough on
me."

"I will be rough no matter what, Leo. Not in my nature to be otherwise." Barzeny started replacing the pieces on the board for a new game. "Now for two dollars I show you interesting version against the Ruy Lopez, something called Spanish Torture in the thirties. Much more interesting than the Najdorf Sicilian you just used."

"For two dollars I should be able to get your drawn game with Tal."

Barzeny smiled and there was a little twinkle behind his eyes. "Masterpiece like that game is worth five times as much . . ."

"So debit my account," Leo said and moved N-KB3. "Wasn't that how it opened?"

"No, no," the Russian emigré said with disdain. "Never I opened with knight. Here is what I did," and he started pushing pieces across the board and explaining his moves. "Sure you have time for this?" he asked.

"I got all night," Leo said and sat back to watch.

Five

LEO TURNED HIS '79 DODGE VALIANT INTO the curb in front of his house and cut the engine. At eleven-thirty at night the town of Harrison was asleep. The streets were empty and the only lights on in the entire block of nondescript two-story frame houses were in Leo's bedroom and in Pete Mancher's living room next door. Sally Mancher was waiting up to guide her inebriated husband to bed with her while Barbara Perkins was already in bed, listening to Johnny Carson.

Oh, the fantasies Leo had on Tuesday nights, which was also Mancher's night out with the boys, of coming home to the wrong house, no television blaring, no littered ashtrays making their home smell like a back-country smokehouse, with a woman waiting for him doing her best to keep her hormones in check. The thought of being someone else for a few hours was intoxicating . . . Mancher had once told him that every drawer pull in their kitchen was different, placed there by his wife who insisted on sensing the nuances in everything she touched. Imagine, Leo had thought, what that meant when the lights were out.

Leo was old enough to understand that fantasies fade under close examination. Besides, Leo valued his family too much to chance playing around. There was Amanda, for whom he'd do anything, and Barbara had her moments when she made him recall the woman he had married. Middle age, Leo reasoned, was a little like a losing basketball season in high school. You kept playing games because they were on the schedule, kept making the same moves and the same excuses for stupid shots, and kept holding your breath for the big win, which always seemed to elude you. But deep down you knew you weren't going to the Nationals and so you settled in for just playing the game and enjoying the occasional three-pointers and once-a-year slam dunk.

Leo locked the car door behind him and headed up the little walkway. The storm door in front of his house was slightly ajar, and he reminded himself again to fix the retracting mechanism, which had been broken since August. Three months was an average gestation time for items on Leo's repair list. He turned his key in the lock and pushed inside. It would take one inspired weekend when there were no invitations to go hunting, no superbowl games, no Clancy novel to finish, and he'd wipe the slate clean. Except, what a slate . . . broken banister rail to the cellar, peeling paint on the kitchen ceiling, a leaky radiator in Amanda's bedroom, a loose dryer switch. It was all getting out of hand, in his lovely two-hundred-and-fifty-thousand-dollar house in the Westchester suburbs which anywhere else would be under one seventy. He shook his head as he laid his coat on the back of the sofa and headed upstairs. Such was the price you paid for a 914 area code.

The first thing he did when he came home on Tuesday nights was look in on Amanda. There was something settling about her room with its confusion of old stuffed animals, rock-and-roll posters, magazine photographs, Hula Hoops, and old arts-and-crafts projects. This was the way it was supposed to be. It didn't matter that there was chipped paint downstairs, this room was perfect. And twelve-year-old Amanda was perfect. He bent down and kissed her lightly on her forehead and watched as she shifted over. He stood still for a moment, hoping she would wake up and say hello, knowing she wouldn't. Then he turned out of the room, closed the door softly, and walked across the hall.

"Hello darling," Barbara said, her eyes still on Carson. A moment later she looked up and asked, "Beat Barzeny tonight?"

"Didn't come close. What'd you have for dinner?"

"Meat loaf. There's still some left. Wait 'til you hear this joke Carson just told. Why is bridge like sex?"

Leo sat down on the queen-size bed and waved his hand to dispel some of the smoke.

"Why?"

"Because in both you need either a good partner or a good hand." She waited, but after ten consecutive losses to some Russian emigré, all Leo was willing to offer was a polite smile.

"Monologue almost over?" he asked.

"Almost, why?"

"Can we talk?"

"Sure, Leo. What about?"

"Florida."

"Again? Do we have to go over that again?"

"I don't know, Barbara. I was thinking on the way home. New York just doesn't seem right anymore. Not for you, not for me, and certainly not for Amanda. This is her future I'm talking about."

"Her future is not in some red-necked southern town," Barbara answered, fixing her eyes back on the set. "I want more for Amanda.'' Leo leaned into the pillows on his side. Another lost game, he thought sadly, even before the opening tip-off.

Six

BARBARA HAD FORGOTTEN TO TELL HIM the night before that the dryer had shorted out. He discovered that early the next morning after he found his shirt drawer empty. This posed a slight problem for him. Selling dining room sets for Rivetz required a decent wardrobe. The customers liked to feel that their salesman knew enough about good dining to distinguish the difference between a shellfish and a dessert fork, and pulling that off wearing a T-shirt was difficult. Leo had three basic suits for work, half a dozen polyester shirts, and enough colorful ties to give him a different look five days a week. Then he had his special things: a soft, three-piece navy-blue woolen suit from Brooks Brothers he had been persuaded to buy for a niece's wedding three years earlier, a couple of 100 percent cotton shirts with French cuffs that needed ironing, and a favorite silk tie Barbara had given him on their tenth anniversary. The special things were only for weddings, first communions, bar mitzvahs, funerals, and theater parties . . . never for work. On one previous occasion when the dryer had shorted out and he had had to wear a cotton shirt for work, it had killed him. One thing Barbara did not do was ironing. Two dollars to the Chinese man to launder his shirt for a normal workday! Grudgingly he broke the seal on the fresh shirt, pulled it on, and then went looking for his cuff links.

If the Brooks Brothers suit and cotton shirt were special, the cuff links were in the realm of the sacred. They were 14-karat yellow gold and had been given to him when he won the all-city interscholastic high school chess competition back in 1963. In the center of each cuff link was a raised chess piece, the king. The cuff links were the most valuable jewelry he owned and made him feel as well dressed as any model in *Uomo*, an Italian magazine displayed on some coffee tables at Rivetz.

"Honey, seen my cuff links?" he shouted with a puzzled expression on his face. "They're not in my top drawer."

His wife was with Amanda, helping with her hair, so he had to ask twice before he got a reply.

"They're in your box, look again."

"They're not." He walked into Amanda's room holding the open leather box. "See?"

She glanced his way and continued with her daughter's hair. "Maybe you mislaid them," she offered.

"Very funny. I use one of these shirts what, three, four times a year? You ever see me put them anywhere but in the box when I take them off?" He looked down again. "I tell you they're not here."

Barbara shrugged. "Amanda?" she said. "Did you take your father's cuff links?"

"What for?" the twelve-year-old replied. "I think they're yucky." There was silence in the room for a moment, then Barbara looked back at her husband.

"You don't think that someone took them?" she asked half jokingly.

"You have any other ideas?"

"Like who, for instance? The Manchers when we had them over for pizza last month? Maybe Barzeny the night you invited him back to play chess all night? Or one of Amanda's girl friends?"

"Or Harmon Parrish," Leo said. "Who comes here once a week."

Barbara didn't reply immediately. She stopped stroking her daughter's hair to face him. "That's absurd," she finally said. "Harmon doesn't need your little gold cuff links. He's a well-known musician, not a petty thief. If you ever saw the way he dresses you'd know how crazy that is.''

"Makes sense to me," Leo said and snapped the box shut.

"What makes more sense is asking your friend Mr. Barzeny. If that man has fifty dollars saved up, I'd be surprised.''

"Stealing cuff links is the last thing Jakob would do." Leo looked down at his daughter. "Amanda, are you sure?''

"Daddy, I never go in your room. Don't worry, they'll probably turn up somewhere.'' She smiled at him. "Are you driving me to school today?''

Leo hesitated for a moment, then turned and walked back across the hall. He took off the shirt, hung it up neatly in his closet, and took down a short-sleeved, open-necked polyester he usually wore in summer. He was burning inside. The cuff links had been stolen, he knew it, and the casual attitude of Barbara and Amanda made him angrier. Okay, so they weren't worth a fortune, but still they were his, in his drawer, in his house. He couldn't pass that off.

"I'll ask Mr. Han if you left them in the cuffs. Maybe he's had them lying around for a few months," Barbara called, in an effort to be a little more helpful.

Fat chance of that, Leo thought. The Chinaman would have called immediately and then returned the cuff links with the shirt. "Stolen," Leo repeated to himself and shook his head.

"Ready Daddy?" Amanda shouted up from the front hall.

"Coming." All right, so he'd try to forget it until tonight and then give the place a thorough search. What else could he do? He smiled at the little girl as he took her hand downstairs. Put it in perspective, he told himself as they headed out the door. How important is it, after all? A simple pair of cuff links. It wasn't as though someone had done something to Amanda.

"Here we are," he said and held out the car door for her. He got in, started up the motor, and pulled away from the curb.

"What are you thinking about, Daddy?" she asked a minute later when they were heading down Archer Street. "You're so quiet.''

"Oh nothing," he lied. "Just looking at the scenery.''

Sure as shit, he thought, the goddamn piano teacher.

* * *

Barbara didn't give the cuff links another thought until later in the afternoon when she was shopping. It was peculiar, she concluded. She couldn't remember hocking them. Never anything of Leo's. The little topaz ring he had given her one anniversary she remembered, and also a little pair of stud pearl earrings, and a gold cigarette lighter. But not the cuff links. Leo would have been furious had he ever found out about her jewelry, especially where the money was going. But she had never dared touch his things simply because she knew he would notice. And now it had happened and she wasn't even the cause of it. So, indeed, where had they gone?

She thought about the cuff links until she came to the baked-goods section and had to make a decision on bread. So many decisions in a supermarket—so many labels to read, so many potentially dangerous ingredients to guard against. It took all one's attention just to buy an uncontaminated loaf of bread. Amanda always liked French toast, and by the time Barbara had selected the least artificial of all the white breads, she had forgotten all about her husband's missing cuff links.

Seven

"HEY, WHAT'S EATING YOU?" SOLLIE asked. "I haven't seen you this quiet since you were working on the twenty-unit dining-room deal at the Crescent Hill Condo complex last year."

Leo looked at his two friends over the lunch table. Henley had his nose buried in the newspaper, but that didn't necessarily mean he wasn't paying attention. "Sorry," he said. "Some little thing at home."

Sollie laughed. "It's always some little thing at home right up until you walk into the lawyer's office. That's the way it was with Maddy and me. The 'some little thing' turned out to be a creep named Lonnie."

"It's nothing like that. It's just that something's disappeared from the house and Barbara's not taking it seriously."

"Like what?" Hanley asked, still reading McAlary's column.

"A pair of cuff links. Barbara thinks I just don't remember where I put them. But she's wrong."

Henley finally looked up and over at Leo.

"You letting a misplaced pair of cuff links ruin a great day?" he said. "I saw you writing up a couple of orders already this morning."

"A mirror and a side chair. Big deal." Leo brushed it off.

"A pair of cuff links?" Hanley repeated.

"Yeah, my only pair in solid gold. You guys don't seem to understand." Leo sounded exasperated. "I know I could get another pair, but I won these in high school. That's not even the point. They were stolen."

"What else did they get?" Hanley said, trying to sound more concerned.

"As far as I can tell, that's all."

"You trying to tell me," Hanley continued, "someone broke into your house and all they got is an old pair of cuff links. Boy, if I was Barbara I'd be pissed. What've you been buying her, brass?"

"Very funny," Leo said. "Besides, no one broke in."

"Oh, an inside job," Sollie said skeptically. "Hey Leo, you know what I think, I think Barbara's right, you probably misplaced them. So, give it time and you'll come across them. Maybe wind up in a sock."

Leo tried to smile but it came out crooked. "Sure."

"See, no big deal," Hanley said and opened his paper once more.

No big deal, Leo thought to himself as he walked back

from lunch five minutes later. Never is until it happens to you.

Eight

BY THE FOLLOWING WEEK, LEO HAD MADE up his mind. The cuff links hadn't turned up even after a four-hour search, Mr. Han hadn't seen them, Barzeny claimed quite accurately that cuff links were the last thing he needed, and the Manchers, Leo recalled, had never been above the first floor during their pizza party. That left, discounting Amanda and her twelve-year-old girl friends, Harmon Parrish. On Tuesday he planned to leave work early and follow Parrish after he left their house. The idea was to find out who Parrish's other students were. With that information, Leo figured, he could start asking some questions.

The only flaw in this plan was that at two forty-five Mr. and Mrs. Frank walked into the store and headed straight for Dining Rooms. They came on like charging buffalo, undeterred by the special sale in Lamps or the new items in the Bargain Bay. A lady with her husband in tow in the middle of the afternoon meant only one thing: They were ready to buy, or in salesman parlance, they were "bagged." Leo, who had been working on Mrs. Frank for more than three weeks to buy the Betsy Ross Heritage Chippendale ten-piece set, found himself staring down the barrel of a six-hundred-dollar commission. He looked at his watch and figured he had it made. He could do the deal easy in forty-five minutes and still make it home in time for the end of Amanda's lesson. Or so he thought.

Before making the purchase, however, Mrs. Frank wanted to impress her husband with the depth and breadth of her legwork. Under normal circumstances Leo would have been pleased, even flattered, at such a bravura performance from a star pupil, but when she started discussing the merits of the glue base of the Betsy Ross Heritage Chippendale collection, he became noticeably fidgety. He had had his order book open for the past thirty minutes, and every time he had picked up a pen, Mrs. Frank had decided to show her husband another feature. What should have been a salesman's dream was becoming Leo's nightmare. With ten minutes left before he had to leave, he figured he had to do something drastic. The Franks were on their knees looking at the locking hardware of the extension leaves under the table.

"Solid brass," intoned Mrs. Frank, "compared to die-cast on the Concord and Lexington Collection imported from Taiwan."

Leo picked up the phone noiselessly. He tapped in Sollie's extension and whispered softly into the phone. Then he sat back to wait. A minute later, as the Franks emerged from under the table and were starting in on the webbing of the seats, Leo's phone rang.

"Yes, Mrs. Coan," he answered in a voice a shade louder than normal. "The Betsy Ross set . . . um," he hesitated . . . "yes, we still have it on the floor." He could see Mrs. Frank perk up her ears. "I have some people looking at it though." Leo glanced at his watch. "Yes, I'll be here for a while." He looked up casually and noted with satisfaction the anguish on Mrs. Frank's face. Three weeks of grinding comparative shopping about to come to naught . . . Christ, they might even have to settle for the Taiwanese stuff. This time she came at him for real.

"We'll take it," she said with the desperation of a Manhattan apartment hunter being shown a large one bedroom with a view. "Henry, give the man a check."

"The Betsy Ross?" Leo said innocently. "The ten pieces?"

"Yeah, the whole megillah," Mr. Frank said resignedly and sat down to do the honors.

In fifteen minutes they were done with the paperwork, and Leo excused himself. The last he saw they were comparing finishes on the table versus the sideboard. He flashed Sollie the thumbs-up sign as he passed and hurried out to his car. If the lights broke right, and with a little luck on traffic, he could still make it home to catch Parrish. The only problem was that goddamn Orantes who had spotted him leaving. He'd have to figure out something creative like a podiatrist appointment. But then he remembered the Franks and he thought, the hell with Orantes. One ten-piece dining room sale per day earned his keep. He started his car and headed for the exit.

Leo had never seen Harmon Parrish before. Barbara had made all the arrangements with him, and Leo's responsibility extended only to paying. He had spoken to him once or twice on the phone and had formed a mental picture of the man Amanda referred to as "that old guy, Parrish." The person who emerged from the front door of his house barely a minute after he had slipped in next to the curb a few doors away certainly did not fit his image. The man had white hair, that was true, but his face looked young enough to make it into one of those mail-order catalogues selling yuppie clothes . . . rugby shirts and skiing underwear and outdoor parkas. Never trust the eye of a twelve-year-old, Leo thought as he watched Parrish get effortlessly into his low-slung car fifty yards away. He waited a moment after Parrish's car pulled away from the curb, then put the Dodge Valiant in gear and followed.

He'd do it just like in the movies, Leo thought as he hung back a few hundred yards from the newer car. He felt oddly exuberant following behind his daughter's piano teacher. He had never done anything quite so theatrical. This is zany, he thought when both stopped for a light in Mamaroneck. Then he spotted Parrish glancing into his rearview mirror and began to worry. Parrish seemed to look into his mirror more than most people. Within five minutes they were in Larchmont where Parrish turned off into the driveway of number 145 Acorn Street. The mailbox at the driveway entrance said EBERHARD. Leo pulled around the corner and put his car in neutral. On a piece of paper he jotted down the name and address, then glanced at his watch. It read four-thirty. The way he figured it, he'd give it another three hours, another three names. That should be enough. He could take the forty-five minutes in which Parrish gave his lessons to grab a quick snack, read the paper, call Barzeny. Unfortunately, he'd have to cancel the chess. He had been planning on bringing Barzeny a corned beef sandwich from Griben's to soften him up. Chess, he concluded reluctantly, could wait a week.

Nine

BARBARA WAS STARING AT LEO ACROSS the den with eyes like two lit Sterno cans, but Leo would not let her anger stop him. He looked down the telephone numbers the directory had yielded for the four names on his list and dialed the first one. Just a few innocent questions, he had told his wife, to see if any of the other houses Parrish taught in had similar occurrences of missing items. "I'll be discreet," he assured her, to which she had shot back, "How in hell can you be discreet with this sort of question?"

"Hello, is this Mrs. Eberhard?" he said in the politest voice he could summon up.

"It is," came the cold reply, and he realized he was already in a hole. Anyone who had to ask that question was grouped immediately into the category of aluminum siding salesmen and magazine subscription agents. Especially at this time of evening. On the defensive, he said immediately, "My name is Leo Perkins and I believe our daughters take piano lessons from the same teacher, Harmon Parrish." He saw his wife's eyes narrow into little slits as the voice on the other end turned mellower.

"Why yes, Mr. Perkins, how are you? Constance speaks often of Amanda. I believe they are in the same class at school this year as well. Constance has Mr. Parrish on Tuesdays. What can I do for you. Is he sick?"

"No, it's not that. I wonder if you could shed some light on something. Actually, this is rather awkward . . ." He turned away from his wife. "You see, we are having our house repainted and just last week I noticed we were missing an expensive piece of jewelry. I wanted to file a claim against the painting company, but before I do that, I have to eliminate anyone else who usually comes into our house. Mr. Parrish is one of the few people who has entry and . . . well, I just wanted to double-check that your family hasn't experienced any similar kind of loss. I'm sure it's the painters, but the insurance company wants me to double-check."

There was a pause on the other end of the line. Finally, Mrs. Eberhard broke the silence.

"Absolutely not, Mr. Perkins. We are not missing anything at all. I would suggest you fire your painters right away."

"Thank you," Leo said meekly. "Sorry to trouble you." He hung up and didn't move for a moment.

"Nothing missing, right?" Barbara sneered. "Just like I told you. Except Harmon is going to find out about it and make our life miserable."

"There are three more names," Leo said quietly.

"This is so embarrassing," Barbara replied and got up and walked out of the room. She returned as Leo finished dialing the next number.

"Hello, is this Mr. Wick? Mr. Wick, my name is Leo Perkins and this is actually a little awkward . . ."

He spun out the same story he had used with Mrs. Eberhard and waited.

"A small glass paperweight?" Leo repeated. "Just kind of disappeared?"

"That's right," Mr. Wick said. "I'm not sure how much it was worth. Had more of a sentimental value. Been in the family for so long no one can remember where it came from. A little millefiori thing. It was upsetting to my wife who has seen these things at Sotheby's go for high prices, but hell, it couldn't have been Parrish. Probably one of the caterers we had for a party couple of months ago. Hell, who knows? Maybe it was one of the guests. But Parrish has been here dozens of times, Mr. Perkins, and that's the only thing that's turned up missing as far as I know."

Leo thanked him and hung up. Barbara watched him as he started in on another number.

"This is insane," she said. "And just about finishes Amanda's lessons with Mr. Parrish. You think it was easy getting him to come to our . . ." she frowned, looking around, ". . . out here?"

"Hello, is this Mrs. Reptash?" Leo continued without a beat. "Oh, when will she be back? That late . . . well maybe you can help me. My name is Leo Perkins and I believe my daughter takes piano with the same teacher as Mrs. Reptash's daughter . . . excuse me, son, that's right, Mrs. Reptash's son. And you are . . . yes, the housekeeper, good, good."

Five minutes later he had her story. An antique silver ashtray and a matching silver cigarette box had mysteriously disappeared three months earlier.

"The madam assumed it was one of the new maids," the housekeeper reported, "so she terminated them both and that was the end of it. Nothing else was ever missing. I'm certain Mr. Parrish doesn't need to pocket other people's keepsakes."

"Thank you. Yes, I'm sure it was the maid."

Leo dialed the last person on his list.

"Conroy residence," he heard as the phone was answered.

"Mr. or Mrs. Conroy, please."

"Whom shall I say is calling?" the voice came back dripping ice.

"Mr. Perkins."

"In regard to what?"

"In regard to a private matter that has nothing to do with selling them anything. If they are busy I can call back."

"I believe they have just finished supper. Please hold on."

Leo breathed out softly. The security at the Conroy residence sounded formidable.

In a moment John Conroy came on the line. He had the kind of voice that would make a room full of CEOs put down their five-year plans and listen. Deep, sonorous, and very impatient.

"Yes, Mr. Perkins, what can I do for you? If it's of a business nature, I handle that at the office."

Leo explained about his problems with the painters again and let Conroy take it from there.

"I hardly think it's Mr. Parrish, sir. He has been in our home several years now giving lessons to both my children. We wouldn't have anyone in our house we didn't think was trustworthy."

"So you have never had anything missing, then? It's what my insurance company needs to know."

"I don't give a damn what your insurance company needs to know. I don't see as what happens in our residence is any of their business."

"No, of course not," Leo backtracked. "I just wanted to eliminate Mr. Parrish from consideration."

"Well, I can do that. He has been coming to this house for years." There was a pause for just a moment. "The fact that we had a minor incident a few months ago with a small Laurencin drawing that was taken out of its frame we traced directly to one of our own people. Bad apples everywhere these days. I told my wife to vet the help more carefully."

"Someone confessed to taking a valuable drawing?"

There was another pause on the other end of the line. "Not exactly confessed. He was a new groom we'd recently hired. We have a stable out back, and every morning the groom comes in to get his orders for the day from Mrs. Conroy. Which horse to saddle up, which saddle, that sort of thing. Passes by the hallway where the drawing was hung. He was a new boy, should have been checked more carefully."

"But he didn't actually say he took it?"

"Of course not, that would have landed him in jail, now wouldn't it? The damn thing was only worth about five thou-

sand dollars, but I couldn't have pilfering going on around
here. We let him go immediately and refused references. But
Mr. Parrish . . . it couldn't have been him. He stays in the
music room, and the drawing disappeared from a back hallway."

"Thank you Mr. Conroy," Leo said slowly. "I guess we
all face the same risks in hiring domestic help these days. It's
so hard to find good ones, I know." He hung up the telephone and rubbed his nose.

"Including us that makes four out of five," he said in the
direction of his wife. "By my book, that's a pretty good
percentage. Ted Williams built a career around a .344."

"I still don't believe it," she said.

"Barbara," he said, trying to sound patient. "You can
stick your head in the sand just so long. The man's a little
pack rat nibbling away at other people's possessions. He depends on just the sort of response you're showing—'Oh, it
couldn't be Mr. Parrish, he's too honorable,' or he's an artist,
or he has good manners, or he's well known. So of course
it's the maid or groom that gets it in the neck while Mr.
Mozart there is free to continue robbing people." He got up
and walked to a window. He looked outside at the lone tree
in his front yard for a moment, then turned around. "But I'll
tell you this, I don't think he's going to be doing it for long,
not if I can help it."

"What are you going to do?" Barbara asked anxiously.

"I'm going to call the cops and have them investigate."

"You wouldn't."

"I sure as hell would. There are a lot of other piano teachers around. The last thing we need is a teacher who's a free-
lance heist artist. Maybe some of his other clients don't care
if some five-thousand-dollar little thing is missing from their
inventories, but I do. Those cuff links were made of real
gold."

"The word will get out that you started this whole thing,"
Barbara said. "It will get around the school."

"Good, let it." The expression on his face was not pleasant. "Tomorrow morning, bright and early," he continued,

"I'll make the call, before he has another day of classes. I think he's done enough damage already."

Ten

LIEUTENANT RUCKER OF THE HARRISON police department had just finished a briefing with two detectives when the phone on his desk rang. He looked at it scornfully for a full six seconds before leaning over and picking it up. To Rucker, all calls spelled disaster. Overdoses, suicides, murders, muggings, immolations . . . everything the depraved mind of man could imagine coursed down the phone lines and spewed out into police precincts everywhere. The size of the precinct didn't matter, the message was always the same. And then the hard part—he'd have to do something about it.

At thirty-one Rucker was the youngest lieutenant in Westchester, and by many accounts, the least deserving. Through concerted ass kissing he had put himself in line for a promotion to sergeant at a time in the mid-eighties when many midlevel police officers were retiring. He distinguished himself in that capacity by filing sloppier arrest reports, alienating more D.A.s, and masterminding more compromised drug busts than any three other sergeants put together. What he was good at, however, was attending fund raisers for assistant county executives, wrangling baseball and basketball tickets for his superiors, and, of course, working late on those nights when he knew they would be in attendance. So naturally, when Lieutenant Mullens retired after a distinguished forty-year career, the police bigwigs looked around and their gaze fell upon their buddy Andrew Rucker, a.k.a. the Scarsdale scalper. In a flash he was once again promoted, thus fulfilling the Peter Principle that one rises to the level of one's own incompetence. What made it worse in Rucker's case was that he had no idea any gulf existed between his abilities and his job description. The fact that he was riding herd on three dozen Harrison police officers and a budget of more than three million taxpayer dollars did not change his style or proclivities. The only difference was that he stopped giving out Knicks tickets and started getting them instead.

Rucker's eyes were the color of molasses and just as lazy, and his mouth was so straight and thin you had to look hard to spot it. But his most prominent feature was his eyebrows, which went just about wall-to-wall from one side of his face to another. His nose was doing its best to divide the line of cover, but it had been outflanked.

"This is Lieutenant Rucker," he said into the phone. "Yeah, who?"

Leo Perkins spoke quietly into the phone. He had read somewhere that police officers respond best when they have responsible, calm witnesses, so he tried to tell the story in as measured and reasonable a voice as possible. It was still early at Rivetz, and he was able to talk without the interruption of the overhead PA system or a dozen browsing clients.

"Give me that name again," Rucker said. "Perkins . . . Leo Perkins."

"Yes." Leo heard some papers rustling on Rucker's desk.

"You wouldn't happen to be the Leo Perkins who owns a green '79 Dodge Valiant, would you?"

Leo frowned. Where the hell was this coming from?

"License plate number AK674?"

"Yes. That's me. I mean, that's my car."

Rucker didn't say anything for a moment. "Where are you calling from?"

"My job. Rivetz Furniture."

"Listen, Perkins, I can send a guy out to pick you up, or you can just make it easy on me and come in . . . say in ten minutes."

"What's this about, my car?"

"I'll tell you when I see you. You know where we are?"

"Over on Rosemont."

"That's it. We'll see you in ten minutes." He hung up and Leo was left staring into the silent phone. Now what, he thought. Barbara was in an accident with the car. He quickly tried his home phone but got no answer. So, maybe she was shopping, he told himself. Orantes was watching him from across the aisle, and as Leo hung up the phone he crossed over.

"Client," Leo said with a smile. "Wants me to check if there's room to bring the new glass-and-concrete Ibiza Collection table into her house. I'll be back in a half hour." He put on his coat and walked a few steps before the section manager said anything.

"You shitting me?"

"If I am," Leo smiled, "you can take away my December draw." After a few more steps he added, "and buy a Big Mac with it," but by then he was far enough away that Orantes didn't hear him. Not that it would have mattered. Orantes had the sense of humor of a seventh-grade math teacher. One laugh a month and then only when no one was looking. A real charmer.

Eleven

BLANKA SOLOGYAR FOUND THE BODY AT seven forty-five that morning when she came to do the cleaning. She had this special arrangement with Harmon Parrish who let her start early while he was still having his breakfast. That made it possible for her to get in three people on

Wednesdays rather than the regular two. A nice man, Mr. Parrish. She'd been with him for several years, but right from the start she could tell . . . all those impressive notices of his concerts on the walls. It was under one of those notices that she had spotted the body, in the hallway between the bedroom and the living room.

Blanka had escaped to the United States in 1956 during the Soviet invasion of Hungary. She had come as a young woman full of hope but also saddened by memories of the murderous treatment of her fellow countrymen. But there wasn't one memory that could have prepared her for what she found in Parrish's apartment that quiet Wednesday morning in November, when sensible people were just rolling out of bed.

His body was propped restfully against the wall as though he were contemplating a ceiling fixture. But what pierced Blanka's eyes was the profusion of color. His uncombed white hair framed his blue agonized face, which sat upon a body drenched in vibrant red. Red, white, and blue, the colors of her adopted country, colors of liberty and justice for all, had been gruesomely co-opted for this still life. And it was, indeed, a very still life. Blanka screamed and ran to the door.

Ten minutes later the police were there, and the little apartment house where Parrish had his rooms started looking like a set for a feature film. There were a half-dozen police cars, the medical examiner's van, the crime-scene lab unit, a morgue truck, a TV station minicam team, and a paramedic unit. By eight o'clock the street had been blocked off and all the early-morning gawkers pushed back.

By the time Rucker arrived they had retrieved the cuff link from next to the body and spotted the scrap of paper in Parrish's jacket pocket. The number AK674 was a tantalizing clue but could mean anything. They'd have to work on it.

The medical examiner placed the time of death around 1:00 A.M. the previous night, which explained why Parrish was dressed in his pajamas. Before the full autopsy they had to rely on the body-temperature gradient, the onset of rigor, and lividity of the skin, and all three bracketed the time as being between twelve and two. Cause of death . . . the M.E. had smiled.

"Take your pick."

Parrish had been garroted. Originally used as a means of execution in Spain, the garrote had been envisioned by its inventors as a mode of death by strangulation. A rope was coiled around the victim's neck and his body lifted off the ground. Very simple and intimate. As styles changed and the rope got thinner, executioners found that it was also doing a decent job of crushing the spinal column, so if they wanted, they could stop just short of death but beyond total paralysis. That came in handy during interrogations. Finally, as the rope became a wire, the victim died not only from lack of air but also from loss of blood to the brain since the wire cut into the soft flesh of the neck and severed everything right down to the bone. Still intimate, but messy. In Parrish's case, very messy.

To the casual observer it looked like Parrish had two mouths. The one on his neck was shaped into a pleasant smile, unlike the contorted one on his face. It was a crescent so sharp that it looked like it had been drawn in with a mechanical pencil, except that out of this curve spilled curtains of red. However fastidious Parrish had been in life, he had made up for it in death. After the crime-scene unit had taken their pictures and measurements, Rucker motioned for the body to be removed. His officers continued a search of the premises while he went to interview Blanka, who was waiting in one of the police cars.

Her hands were shaking and she was smoking a cigarette as if it was a straw. "You want some coffee?" he asked as he slid into the seat next to her, but she just shook her head.

"I want to go home, that's all," Blanka whimpered. "Call my other people and tell them I can't come today. Holy Mother. Who would have thought I'd ever see such a thing."

"I have to ask you some questions," Rucker said. "You ready?"

She nodded.

He asked her about how long she'd been working for Parrish, and about what kind of a guy he was, and if she'd ever seen anyone in the apartment, or if she'd ever spotted anything suspicious around, or if he ever made any comments about enemies, and a dozen other questions that were standard in a murder investigation. Breathlessly, one after the other, putting her through the paces and only letting her come up for air when he asked her to give an opinion.

"Who do you think killed him?"

To which she took a moment to collect herself and said, "How would I know? I just worked for him, that's all, four hours a week."

Rucker leaned back into the seat and looked at the activity around him. It was a minute before he spoke again. "But you had a key, right? You let yourself in. See, we have a problem, Blanka, the door wasn't forced. Whoever killed him either had a key or Parrish himself must have opened the door."

Blanka Sologyar didn't hesitate. "Maybe, but if you're wondering if I ever gave my key to anybody, the answer is no," she said righteously. "I got ten keys of the places I work and I take care of them. I never let them out to nobody."

"Okay," the lieutenant said and tried a new tack. "Remember anything unusual about Parrish?"

"Officer, there's something unusual about all my clients, they pay me on time. That's why I got them. Other than that," she shook her head, "nothing that I could tell. In the morning while I was working he'd play his piano and go out around eleven. He'd get phone calls but I'd never listen in. I have to hurry on Wednesday, I got two other people, so I wasn't used to hanging around there when the place was clean."

Rucker jotted down something in his notebook and closed ,t with a snap.

"The officers have your address?" he asked her.

"Yes, I gave it to them."

"We'll be in touch," he said and got out of the patrol car. "You can go now." He looked at his watch and decided to head back to his office. Not much else he could do at the scene. His people were already working on Parrish's car, and some of the others were canvassing the neighbors. He was heading toward his own vehicle when he heard his name being called. Officer Nelson came running over with a sheet of music from Parrish's car, one with a torn corner that seemed to match the scrap of paper they had found in his jacket. *Number of car tailing me* was scrawled right next to the ripped corner. Good, Rucker thought, now we're getting somewhere. He called in the number on the scrap of paper and in less than a minute had the car and the owner. Thank God for computers. Forty-five minutes later, when he had finally settled in at his desk, he got Leo Perkins's call. What a coincidence, he thought. Must be my goddamn lucky day.

Twelve

RUCKER WASN'T GIVING ANYTHING AWAY, even after Perkins's ten-minute story. Leo studied his face, but he could read more from a Chinese newspaper than he could from the policeman's features. It was a face made for late-night poker games.

"It's funny," Rucker said. "You coming in with that story about Parrish." He said it in a tone that made Perkins uneasy.

"Why's that?" Leo said. "Had other complaints about him?"

Rucker thought that one over for a moment before answering. "I wish we had. Apparently someone had a complaint against him but took it private. Last night Parrish was murdered." He watched as the color drained from Leo's face. "Garroted, sliced clean through two arteries and his throat. He was found by his maid this morning on the floor in a pool of blood.'' He looked at his watch. "Three hours ago.''

It took a minute until the shock wore off and Leo found his voice.

"Murdered?''

"Very.'' Rucker leaned forward in his chair. "We haven't finished looking through his apartment yet or talking to his neighbors, but we did find this.'' He opened his hand and a scrap of paper fell out onto the table. Leo picked it up and found himself staring at his license-plate number, AK674.

"What's this?''

"A piece of paper torn from some sheet music. You have any idea what it was doing in his jacket pocket?''

Leo shook his head. "No.''

"Perhaps it would help if I showed you the piece it was torn from. We found it in his car.'' He bent down and pulled something out of a bag on the floor. It was the sheet of music for Debussy's "Claire de Lune'' except that a corner was ripped away and there were some words scribbled near the tear. Leo leaned closer.

Suddenly it hit him. He felt lightheaded, as though the force of gravity had been suspended in his vicinity. He had been spotted by Parrish while he was tailing him, spotted, and his license written down, and now this son-of-a-bitch cop was asking him all about it.

"Were you following him?'' Rucker asked flat out. "Or was it just your car?''

If that was Rucker's idea of a joke, Leo wasn't amused. He thought quickly about his options. They boiled down to clamming up and getting a lawyer, or telling the truth. Telling the truth was cheaper.

"I told you I got the names of his other students from my daughter.'' He fidgeted. "That's not exactly true. I did that by following him when he left my house.''

"When was that?''

"Yesterday. He must have noticed me.'' Leo shrugged. "It's not illegal to follow someone in your car, is it?''

Rucker leaned back but didn't say anything. He just

watched Leo with his camouflaged eyes. Leo could hear the traffic outside the window on Rosemont and the steady clatter of a typewriter somewhere down the hall. Rucker's silence was getting on his nerves, and now Rucker had picked up a pencil and started tapping it on the edge of his desk. Like little tacks in his brain . . . tap, tap, tap, tap. Leo wished he was back at Rivetz, back behind his desk where the only thing you could be accused of was giving a customer too low a price.

The beat continued. Tap, tap, tap, tap. It was like a bad movie from the thirties with Claude Rains or George Raft.

"Perhaps there is something else in your story," Rucker finally said, "that might not be strictly truthful. Want to review it again?"

"Everything else is just like I told you," Leo said. His voice sounded shaky even to him, although Leo sensed it was dangerous to appear scared. "I was annoyed about my cuff links and wanted to see if he had stolen from other houses. It's clear now that he had."

"Maybe," Lieutenant Rucker said. "And maybe not. Maybe that's just a convenient explanation for the presence of your cuff link in his apartment."

Leo raised his eyes.

"Yes, we found them . . . or rather we found one of them, exactly as you described." He reached into his pocket and removed a little plastic baggie which he placed on the table in front of his visitor. Leo didn't have to open it to spot his cuff link with the replica of the chess piece in gold relief. "I thank you for saving us some trouble in tracking it down. It has a maker's stamp, and a date. It would have been difficult but not impossible. But I repeat, we only found one even though we combed through the apartment for the mate."

Between his anger and his fear, Leo had a hard time getting the words out. "Where did you find it?"

"Next to the dead man's hand," Rucker said and let that sink in for a minute. "In such cases, the simplest theory is the best. Nine out of ten homicide detectives would say Parrish struggled with his murderer and in grappling with him, came away with his cuff link. Makes sense, don't you think? If not, where was the other one?'' He sat back and a smug grin came over his face. ''Listen, Perkins, we've only started this investigation, but I would say at the moment, you are squarely in the middle of it. You want to tell me, for example, where you were last night between twelve and two A.M.?''

''At home in bed,'' he answered quickly. ''Where I suppose more than three-quarters of Westchester County was.''

''Witness?''

''I'm afraid my wife was asleep at that hour. I was reading. We both went upstairs around eleven.''

''Ummm,'' Rucker said. ''Too bad.''

''What the hell is this?'' Perkins asked, finally unbottling his anger. ''I come in here trying to help the police apprehend a thief who has been stealing for years and I get put on the spot and asked a bunch of crap . . . just because I followed him for a couple of hours, or because you found one of the cuff links I voluntarily reported missing. Lay off, huh? Next question you ask goes through my lawyer.'' He got up. ''I'm going. You got any objections to that? If so, arrest me and read me my rights.''

Rucker looked up at him and smiled. ''No,'' he said. ''You're free to go. Just not too far, that's all.''

''Thanks.''

''And Perkins,'' Rucker added. ''That probably was a good idea about the lawyer. You never know when you might say something incriminating.'' He winked, but with his heavy eyebrows it came out looking more like a sneer.

Thirteen

WORD OF PARRISH'S DEATH MADE IT
onto the six o'clock news as a small item: "Westchester
piano teacher found murdered." The producers in Manhattan were not taken in by Harmon's inflated curriculum vitae,
the Bogardus Fellowship notwithstanding. Vladimir Horo-
witz he wasn't, but to many people in Westchester, his death
came as an item of interest. Besides his thirty weekly lessons,
there were a half dozen community centers and libraries
around the county that could no longer count on Harmon
Parrish to give concerts for what better-known pianists considered gratuities. A musical light in the community, albeit
low wattage, had been extinguished, and his passing was
certainly commented upon.

Amanda took it better than her mother. She knew that
sooner or later, someone else would fill his role. She had, of
course, the shock of disbelief when her father told her that
someone she knew had been murdered, but her horror was
soon replaced by the giddy knowledge that, at least for a few
weeks, she could forget about her piano practice.

Barbara, however, was greatly shaken when Leo told her
the gruesome news. She sat, unmoving, for several minutes,
until Leo thought it best to leave her alone without telling
her of his own problem. He had little doubt that as soon as
Rucker started investigating Parrish, he'd be off the hook.
Still, maybe it wasn't a bad idea to get a lawyer. Trouble
was, he had no idea who to get. His eyes wandered over to
the Yellow Pages under their night table, but then he con-

vinced himself that was crazy. Another day or so and Rucker would apologize, he was sure of it. So he lay back on the bed and tried to relax, maybe go to sleep. Barbara found him like that an hour later, his eyes still wide open, trying to fight his way out of this daytime nightmare.

Fourteen

SERGEANT NELSON KNOCKED POLITELY ON the door of number 135 Overton Street and waited for a response. Big case, he thought proudly, don't blow these interviews. The fact that Rucker had thrown the background investigation his way and not to that moron Santini pleased him enormously. Besides, adjudicating family disputes paled in comparison to an honest-to-goodness murder investigation. Nelson was a little man, with a dark little moustache and a stomach that made for a difficult follow-through in bowling. But in his police uniform he cut a pretty convincing picture. He had little humor and not much more imagination, but an abundance of doggedness. In the league he played in he was considered a good cop.

The house was a modest, two-story frame dwelling with a five-year-old American compact car sitting in its driveway. Nelson glanced over his shoulder at Leo Perkins's house across the street and tried to see if anyone was looking. The only person home at 11:00 A.M. would be Perkins's wife, but there was no movement behind any of the windows facing the street. He heard a scraping behind the door in front of him and turned in time to see it move inward and a somewhat puzzled face appear in the small opening. A chain kept the door connected to the jamb in case the woman's visitor turned out to be Conan the Barbarian. Nelson flashed his badge and waited until she unlocked the door further.

"The police?" the woman said. "What'd I do?"

"I just need some information, Mrs. Pinsky. Can I come in?"

She pulled back and opened the door, and watched as he passed her. She followed and motioned to her living room, a collection of final-sale items from several discount furniture outlets with the same unifying theme: Mediterranean Modern. The paintings on the wall were just as dreary.

"Mrs. Pinsky, I've spoken to some of your neighbors, and I wanted to confirm what they had to say about Mrs. Perkins."

"The woman across the street?"

"That's right."

"What about her? I don't usually pay much attention . . ."

Nelson opened a small notebook and checked something. "I understand," he continued, "that on Tuesdays their daughter took piano lessons. Mr. Perkins told me they began at three-thirty. I was wondering if you could tell me what time the teacher usually got to the house?"

"This is about that Harmon Parrish thing, isn't it?" The woman gave Nelson a look a fox would have envied. It seemed to fit perfectly on her face, which itself looked like Mediterranean Modern—lots of cheap makeup over a formless structure. "The guy that was murdered two days ago?"

Nelson nodded. "When did he usually arrive?"

"Well, now, I don't usually hang around here taking surveys."

"I understand."

"But if he arrived later than three oh-nine every Tuesday I'd be surprised." She winked at him and Nelson got the feeling she probably could give chapter and verse of the interior life of the Perkins family.

"And Amanda?"

"The daughter . . . never before three twenty-five, on the big yellow school bus. Sometimes the piano teacher even got there say around two fifty." This was to make her first wink more pointed.

"So they had a lot of time alone," Nelson said. "Did you ever see them outside together, Mrs. Perkins and Parrish?"

"What would they be going outside for? I suspect what they had to do was strictly an indoor activity." She grinned now quite openly. "Mind you, I don't have anything against the woman 'cept maybe she's a little high-and-mighty now and then. This is Harrison, remember, and the way she walks around with her nose in the air not talking to anyone, you'd think we were living in Fairfield County. But the husband seems to be a regular guy, hard-working."

"Did he ever come back early on a Tuesday lesson?"

"Ho, that would have been rich," Mrs. Pinsky said. "Never, not until this week anyway. I saw him drive up around four or a little after. He pulled his car over on my side of the street, which was unusual, and stayed inside. I noticed that when the piano teacher took off, he took off after him."

Nelson hesitated for moment, then asked a final question. "Did Mrs. Perkins see any other . . . um . . . men in the house alone on a regular basis?"

"No, far as I could tell Parrish was the only one, but then I told you, I wasn't taking a survey now, was I."

"No, certainly not, Mrs. Pinsky." He got up and started for the door.

She cleared her throat. "The other neighbors around here say the same thing?"

"Just about," Nelson said with a smile. "You're not the only one around here not doing surveys." He pulled the front door closed behind him and headed across the street.

Whether she had been watching him was impossible to tell, but Barbara Perkins answered her bell even before he brought his hand back to his side. Nelson stepped inside.

"I expected the police," she said. "It was such a brutal, senseless thing." She looked a lot better than she had the night before when Leo had told her. Nelson looked carefully but there wasn't even a hint of redness around the eyes. Not that there had to be, Nelson thought. Hell, these women have affairs all the time with as much concern as if they were trying on new dresses. Christ, Marie Capiletti in his bowling league had already confessed to three of them.

"Mind if I ask you a few questions? I understand you were one of Mr. Parrish's clients."

Barbara nodded and pointed to the dinette table in the kitchen. "Can I get you a cup of coffee?" she asked.

"No thanks," he answered. "This won't take long."

"What would you like to know?" she asked after they were both seated.

Nelson shrugged. "What he was like. Anything you think might help us in our investigation. Like, did he ever mention he was having problems or had people on his back?"

She shook her head. "Never. You have to understand, Officer, that I didn't usually talk to him too much. He'd come, give Amanda a lesson, get paid, and go. I was usually puttering around in the little greenhouse we have in the back."

So that's how it's going to play, Nelson thought and smiled to himself. With a book full of witnesses it would be easy to break that story when the time came.

"Did he seem nervous or edgy when he came for the lesson this week?" Nelson asked and let his eyes trail around the kitchen. She noticed but stuck to the question.

"Not that I could tell."

"Was he ever strapped for money, like, did he ever ask you for advances or anything?"

She shook her head. "He never looked like he needed money," she said. "I always thought he dressed nicely."

I'll bet you did, Nelson told himself, but what he said was, "Did Amanda ever take a lesson at his place?"

"No, he always came here."

Nelson's eyes were still dancing around, and he finally spotted what he wanted.

"So you never saw Parrish outside of your house . . . I mean you and Amanda."

There was only the slightest hesitation. "No, never."

"And is this Amanda?" Nelson said and got up and walked to a shelf on the far wall. On top of it was a bunch of pictures in cheap plastic frames, each one containing a picture of Leo, Amanda, or Barbara, or some combination. He picked up one of them and brought it down.

"Yes, that's Amanda."

Nelson studied it for a moment and put it back. As he did he knocked another of the frames over. "Sorry," he said and put it upright. "And this is your husband?"

"Yes."

"Nice-looking family," Nelson said and turned back to face her. "I guess that's all for now. We might have more questions when new things develop." He headed toward the door and was about to open it when he turned back.

"Oh, by the way, did you know that your husband followed Mr. Parrish from your house two days ago, followed him for about three hours?"

Barbara glared at him with eyes that could have cut through quarter-inch steel.

"I told him not to. I told him it was crazy."

"He should have listened," Nelson said and turned through the door. Barbara Perkins didn't move for several minutes, and when she did it was not in the direction of the kitchen. Under normal circumstances she'd have missed the small picture in its plastic heart-shaped frame that was now in Nelson's pocket. But under the present circumstances, she strode into the living room to pour herself a stiff drink.

Fifteen

RUCKER HANDED THE PICTURE BACK TO Sergeant Nelson on their way to the M.E.

"Good work," he said. "Get me a blowup and put it with the head shot we got from Parrish's apartment. I want you and Gonzales and Santini to cover every little two-bit flea-bag motel and cocktail lounge in a ten-mile radius. I'm betting she didn't keep it to twenty-minute sessions. Hell, that's not even enough time for decent foreplay."

They turned the corner and walked down to Dr. Ingrahm's office. Ingrahm had been the Westchester County medical examiner for twenty-five years, and there wasn't too much he hadn't seen. One wall of his office was crammed with forensic medicine manuals while the other three held plaques, degrees, photographs, and the general honorary residue of a lifetime spent in civic service. There was a skull and some assorted bones on a side table that he kept, he said, to demonstrate forensic points to young assistant district attorneys. Rucker was convinced he kept them purely for atmosphere. Ingrahm, if he was anything, was a showman, and walking into his office was a little like walking into a regional theater doing a one-man play. Working with the dead so long, Ingrahm looked forward to a live audience. They didn't even bother knocking on his door before pushing through.

Ingrahm didn't look up from the computer screen he was working at. He shifted his eyes from the screen to a hand-written report on his desk, then back again, and pecked a few keys.

"The hell with modernization," he grumbled. "Takes me twice as long to file a goddamn report now I got this damn thing." He looked up finally and saw Rucker and Nelson easing themselves into his only two empty chairs. "Well, if it ain't Henry the Fourth and Falstaff," he said. "What can I do for you boys?"

"Parrish," Rucker said.

"Yeah, I thought so. I'm just finishing that up now. Used to be I could file a handwritten report, but no, that's no goddamn good anymore." He hit a few more keys, then pressed a button on the machine that made it flash something on the screen and produce a noise like an old 45 record changer. "Progress!" He leaned back in his desk chair and looked at Rucker with cold, lifeless eyes. Twenty-five years of examining bloody mutilated bodies took something out of a man, and in Ingrahm's case it was the color from his eyes. The rest looked normal, but the eyes were almost transparent.

"What specifically was it you were interested in?" he asked. "I know you boys don't read these things word-for-word. Takes me five goddamn hours to do the autopsy, another three to type it up, and you guys invariably cut to the bottom line."

"The garrote," Rucker said, "is kind of an unusual way to kill someone. Ever see it before?"

"Aside from death by uncontrollable laughter, there's not much I haven't seen." He reached over and lifted a cigarette out of a pack that was lying on his desk. He lit it, took a deep drag, and began coughing uncontrollably. After twenty seconds he got hold of himself.

"Goddamn cigarettes will kill you," he said. He took another drag, which seemed to settle him down.

"Anything you can help me with? You know what I'm looking for," Rucker said.

"Yeah, chestnuts," Ingrahm said. "Plucked right out of the fire. But this time you're in luck. These hands-on murders are always more fun to reconstruct. Knife killings, blunt-instrument attacks, strangulations—murderer always leaves some kind of calling card. In this case, the murderer left a stack of them.''

Rucker leaned forward. "Yeah, like what?"

"Angle of the wire incision on the neck for one. It plotted out to sixteen degrees off horizontal." Ingrahm pulled out a fresh piece of paper from his desk and drew a profile of a head with the neck attached. Then he drew a line horizontally across the neck and another line above it at an angle. "Like this. Did you get to see the murder instrument?"

"A piece of wire," Nelson said, "like from a piano."

Ingrahm stabbed his cigarette into an ashtray that looked like it hadn't been emptied in a month, opened a manila envelope, and withdrew a coiled piece of wire. Each end of the wire had a short piece of wood attached. What looked like dried blood coated a one-foot length in the middle.

"A G-sharp string to be exact," the doctor said. "Twenty thousandths of an inch thick and when tightened around someone's neck, just like it's name," Ingrahm said. "Chopin wrote the impossible Double Thirds Etude in G-sharp, and everyone thought that was a killer."

"Spare me the concert notes," Rucker said and reached out and lifted it up. "Anything the lab could work up?"

"The blood checked out to be Parrish's. No fingerprints on the handles," Ingrahm said, "some microscopic smudges of synthetic rubber on the wood, probably from gloves. Handles look like they were cut from a standard broomstick. The wire is attached through a quarter-inch stainless eyehook screwed into the wood. It's a homemade job, not the kind of item you can pick up at your local Sears hardware department." Ingrahm chuckled but Rucker and Nelson weren't joining in.

"Now," he said, standing up, "Let me demonstrate." He took the wire in his hands and placed a loop of it over Sergeant Nelson's head, thus assuring his full attention. "Please stand," he said. Nelson stood.

"Now, you're about five seven, right?"

"Seven and a quarter," the sergeant answered.

"But who's counting," Ingrahm added in his gravelly voice. "Anyway, about the same height as your victim. Now,

Parrish was garroted from behind, and the way the murderer did it was probably like this . . .'' Ingrahm thrust his elbows to the side and pretended he was pulling outward. ''The way to get the most force is to place your hands right in front of your chest. You'll notice that the wire forms an angle on Sergeant Nelson's neck much lower than the one I've drawn at sixteen degrees. Now, I'm five eleven. So by a simple calculation, knowing that the murderer's hands were sternum height and knowing body proportions, it's fairly easy to give him an accurate height . . . which I've calculated in my report as six foot three inches.'' Dr. Ingrahm winked. ''Give or take an inch.'' He removed the wire from around Nelson's neck, to his immense relief. A tiny smile creased the corners of Rucker's face. He was thinking of having to look up to talk to Perkins. ''What else?'' the lieutenant asked.

Ingrahm went back to his cluttered desk and placed the garrote back in its envelope. Then he placed it to one side, dropping it between two half-empty coffee cups and directly on top of a stack of daily chess columns from the *New York Times*.

''You'll love this,'' he said, reaching for another cigarette. ''I measured the depth of the cut on both sides of the neck. To my surprise they came out the same.'' He looked up at Rucker with his colorless eyes as if he had just discovered $E = MC^2$. He lit the cigarette, but this time his lungs were prepared, and he only gave one protesting cough.

''You want to explain?'' Rucker asked tiredly. ''Some of us aren't as expert on wound depth as you.''

''It's quite simple,'' the M.E. said. ''Usually in a garroting, one hand being stronger than the other, one side of the wound is deeper than the other. In this case they were the same, which indicates that the murderer has equal strength in his hands, a pretty good indication that he is ambidextrous.''

Nelson whistled. ''Ain't science grand,'' he said happily.

''And finally,'' Ingrahm continued, ''from the actual depth of the cut, my guess is that the person you are looking for is one strong son of a bitch. He exerted enough force on that wire to cut down through close to ten millimeters of entwined veins and arteries, muscle tissue, and throat cartilage. This is not some tall girl scout you're looking for.''

Rucker nodded. "I didn't think so. Thanks, Doctor. I always find our meetings so . . . educational.'' He started to stand up.

"I'll bet you do," Ingrahm said. "Saves you the trouble of reading the goddamn report. There's one more thing I thought you'd like to know, Lieutenant. Parrish was a cocaine user. My guess is he did maybe half a gram to a gram a day. Blood vessels in his nose showed signs of continued chronic use.'' Ingrahm looked at him with a wry smile. "Thought it might add an interesting little note to things. It might even change your case.''

"I don't think so," Rucker answered. "These days I suppose you can find traces of cocaine up anybody's nose.''

"I didn't say traces," Ingrahm corrected. "I said up to a gram a day. You want the garrote?'' Ingrahm held it out.

"One more thing," the lieutenant said. "Were there signs of a struggle? Any skin fragments or hair or blood under Parrish's nails?''

Ingrahm stated formally, "No, they were clean.''

"Isn't that unusual, I mean in a killing where the murderer is so close to his victim?''

Ingrahm didn't answer right away. "He'd have several seconds to respond, maybe ten to twenty before he lost consciousness," he said finally. "But it does seem like enough time to make contact.'' He shrugged.

"Thanks anyway," Rucker said and motioned to Nelson. When they were back outside in the corridor he gave the sergeant another job.

"Find out if Perkins is righty or lefty.''

"How the hell am I going to do that?'' Nelson said.

"You'll figure something out. And maybe if we're real lucky, we'll find out he's both.'' Rucker smiled. "And then we'll be home free.''

Sixteen

PILAR EBERHARD, CONSTANCE'S MOTHER, looked past the aft cockpit guardrails and up to the main house. The Hinkley sixty-four-foot ketch rose and fell lightly against the dock with the movement of the inlet's gentle swells. Her spring lines were off but she was still tied securely, bow and stern, awaiting their last passenger. Pilar looked at her watch for the fifth time since ten o'clock, when Amanda was supposed to have arrived. So inconsiderate of them to be late, she thought, but then what did you expect from people who didn't have a sailboat? They had no understanding of catching a tide at its ebb or the fickleness of a gentle November northwester. She looked over at Constance, who was reading a Nancy Drew book on the cabin coach roof, and shrugged. Well, it had been a promise to her daughter so now she had to live with it. That's what happened when you sent your children to public school, even if it happened to be in an area with an average per-household income of over $70,000. Someone was always sneaking into your family circle with the wrong credentials. She had tried to explain to Constance that even though Amanda was in her class and took piano lessons with Harmon Parrish, they came from different backgrounds and might not make such good friends. And where had it gotten her? With an extra guest for what was supposed to be a glorious day of surprisingly warm November sailing, probably the last sail of the year before Bradford put the boat up. An extra guest who was now twenty minutes late. She could tell from the fact that her husband

58

was checking the hanks on the big Genoa for the third time that his patience, a commodity he had precious little of, had worn thin. She sighed again. What one does for children . . .

Pilar got up and checked the port foresail sheet and the Lewmar winch it was loosely coiled around. She was a small woman, five foot two in her impeccably appropriate Sperry Topsiders, with an athletic grace to her movements around the deck that complemented her still-tanned, attractive face. She moved over to check the traveler and was about to check the main sheet when she heard the little girl's voice calling from the dock.

"Sorry we're late everyone, Daddy had to search everywhere for the Dramamine," Amanda announced. She tossed a small canvas bag onto the boat and climbed over the guardrail. "Hi, Constance, I brought some magazines."

"Yes, sorry," Leo said, standing on the dock. "But I didn't think you wanted a twelve-year-old invalid on board. She tends to get sick on moving vehicles."

"Coming with us, Mr. Perkins?" Bradford Eberhard asked as he reached up to adjust the telltale eight feet up on the port stay. "It's not that we need an extra hand, Pilar and I have sailed this thing up to Nova Scotia alone."

Leo easily turned aside their insincere invitation. This particular Saturday he was filling in on a ten to three o'clock shift and was already late. Afterwards he'd promised himself a late-afternoon session at McArdle's to make up for the Tuesday night he'd missed.

"Thank you, but not today. I'll pick Amanda up this afternoon."

"After five," Mrs. Eberhard said. "By the way, did you ever find that piece of jewelry you were missing?"

Leo hesitated, remembered the phone call, then shook his head. "We think it was the painters."

"Isn't it always?" she said. She turned the key on the big diesel and the engine started flawlessly. "You mind throwing me the lines?"

Leo unwrapped the docking lines and swung them onto the boat. Constance's mother snapped the boat into gear.

"Have a good day," she called as the Hinkley slipped out

of its berth and turned left toward Long Island Sound. When the boat was about two hundred yards offshore Bradford started winching the main halyard, and a blindingly white expanse of dacron sail rose above the boat. Leo waved for another few seconds, then turned and headed for his car. Yeah, so there were yachts in Florida too, he thought. Plenty of them.

Leo didn't get twenty feet inside the door before Orantes hit him with his little speech. So he had missed two browsers . . . big deal. Isn't that what section managers are supposed to do anyway, cover when someone is sick or late? By the time Orantes finished ranting about his lack of responsibility and dedication to Rivetz Furniture Inc., another browser had come and gone.

"If I had the power, I'd fire you tomorrow," Orantes concluded.

"What's wrong with today?" Leo asked.

Orantes gave him a black look. "Okay, so maybe I can't fire you, but one thing I can do is write you the worst evaluation since the invention of the pencil. If you want to get anywhere in this organization, you'd better shape up."

"Yes sir," Leo said and saluted. "Sorry sir. It won't happen again, sir."

Orantes let Leo's needling pass and nodded behind him to the warehouse. "The new Carrara marble table finally came in last night." His face lost its anger. "God, it's beautiful."

"Yeah, and weighs three tons. Why the hell did they ever order it?" Leo asked.

"Because when I saw the picture I told them that we had a market for it. Plenty of people come in and ask for big marble tables."

"That seat twelve?" Leo shook his head. The Carrara table had been long in coming and was a much-discussed item among the salesmen. Most of them agreed that it was the biggest white elephant since San Simeon and would attract about as many buyers. Except that Orantes had fallen in love with the behemoth and was planning to bring it into the middle of the Dining Room showroom space with the new Christmas displays—a horrible idea to people whose livelihood depended on selling things. One very expensive thirty-six-square-foot polished slab of marble meant two fewer American Heritage tables, their biggest movers. But Orantes controlled display, and now that the rock of Gibraltar, as it had come to be known, had arrived, it was guaranteed center stage within a few weeks.

"Don't you want to take a look at it?" Orantes asked. His eyes fairly shone. "Marble legs, too."

"I can wait," Leo said and moved over toward his desk. He took off his jacket and sat down heavily. He was still thinking of what an absolute jerk Orantes was when Hanley sauntered over.

"I noticed the two of you stroking each other again," Hanley said.

"Something like that."

"Be careful of him, Leo. Those mini-management guys got no real power so they take it out elsewhere. I don't trust him."

"Yeah, so what else is new?"

Hanley sat himself down on the edge of the desk. The way he was being so nonchalant, Perkins figured something was up.

"Someone came by asking about you earlier." He hesitated. "A cop."

Leo's back stiffened but he tried to sound casual. "Yeah, so what'd he want to know?"

"General stuff. How long I've known you. What you were like. Did you get along with your wife? An older guy, kind of balding. Little moustache."

"Shit!"

"You in any trouble?" Hanley asked.

"I don't know," Leo said. "The cops have some crazy idea I'm involved with this Harmon Parrish thing. I can't believe they're still at it."

"Well, I guess they are. I didn't tell him anything specific. Then he asked me the craziest thing—whether you played baseball."

"Baseball?"

"Yeah, but I didn't tell him about the company softball league. Then he asked me if I knew if you were left-handed, or what?"

Leo rubbed his forehead. "I don't believe this."

"But you don't have to worry about it, at least from my side. I can't say anything about the others. He must of been here for an hour and the last guy he spoke to was," Hanley pointed, "Orantes."

"The son of a bitch didn't say a thing to me about it."

"Yeah, like I told you, I wouldn't turn my back on him even in a room full of mirrors. I think you got a problem there."

"I think," Leo said slowly, "you may be right."

Seventeen

IT WAS FIVE-THIRTY WHEN LEO RETURNED to the Eberhards' to pick up his daughter. Barzeny was in the car with him, the two men still discussing their last game, which had taken all of twenty minutes to play but which would take over an hour to analyze. From McArdle's to the Eberhards' was over twenty minutes, which meant an additional forty minutes round trip in which Leo could convince Barzeny that even though he had lost the game, his strategy had been correct, save for one little misstep.

"Is okay, I wait in car," Jakob said softly as they pulled down the long driveway. "You go in. Big houses give me nervous condition. Better to look at big trees." Leo hopped out.

The big sailboat was securely moored out back, and the

house was awash in light. Neither Bradford nor Pilar was there to greet him. A maid opened the door and showed Leo into the living room while she went to fetch Amanda. Leo looked around casually at the modern furniture, oddly amused that here was an entire house filled with furniture, none of which had ever seen the inside of a Rivetz discount store. He patted the sofa. Its leather was so soft it felt like silk, and the end tables had been joined so intricately Leo doubted there was a staple or piece of metal in the two of them. The door opened and the maid reappeared.

"Amanda says she'll be down in a few minutes. They're listening to one last song on Constance's CD player."

Leo smiled at her and expected to see her go back to whatever parlor maids usually do at five-thirty on a Saturday afternoon. When she didn't budge, he found it exceedingly awkward. After another minute he couldn't restrain himself. "You needn't worry," he said, his smile melting into a scowl. "I don't intend to steal the ashtrays."

"Oh, it's not that," Theresa said haltingly. "I wanted to tell you something . . ."

Leo closed his eyes. "Amanda broke something?"

The young woman shook her head. She had a pink face and eyes the color of a County Cork meadow in June. "No, and if she did I couldn't care less. It's about Mr. Parrish. I know your daughter used to take lessons from him like Constance." She moved closer and started worrying her hands together. "He was murdered, I read, and the police have been around here asking questions, even of me." Leo watched her closely, but she looked away. "I didn't tell them about the note I found, but Mrs. Eberhard did, I'm sure of it." Now she looked back at him and for the first time, her face looked strained. "Your daughter's a nice girl, and I wouldn't want anything to happen to her that you weren't prepared for."

"What note?" Leo asked.

Theresa hesitated for a moment, deciding where to go with it.

"Parrish was not all that innocent," she said finally. "I

mean, he was . . . not what he seemed. Believe me, I know. Maybe your wife got caught.''

''What note?'' Leo asked again, this time taking a step toward the woman. Her eyes darted to the floor, then came back up steadily.

''Well, I was cleaning in the music room the day after he was killed, and I found this piece of paper on the floor under the piano bench. Constance had just had a lesson two days earlier, and no one besides her usually goes in there. Her mother sometimes with fresh flowers, but no one else. The note wasn't in anybody's handwriting I knew so I just had a little glimpse at it . . . I figured it must have fallen out of Parrish's pocket or briefcase when he came to the lesson.''

''It was from Parrish?''

''To him. I can't remember exactly what it said, but it started off, 'Harmon,' then something like . . . 'surely our romance is too risky.' '' She paused. ''It was signed Barbara. I knew that was your wife's name from Amanda.''

Leo sat down on the couch slowly, in his confusion unaware of its creamy softness. Of course it could be any Barbara, but seeing as how Amanda's lesson came right before Constance's . . .

''What did you do with the note?'' Leo asked.

''I was going to throw it out when I turned and saw Mrs. Eberhard coming in with a vase of flowers. She saw me holding the note and asked what it was.'' Theresa shrugged. ''I gave it to her.''

Barbara and Parrish? Leo couldn't begin to imagine it.

''And knowing her, I think she probably showed it to the police officer that came early this morning,'' Theresa added. ''Mrs. Eberhard can be very . . . thoughtless.'' The maid took a step away. ''I figured you should know about it.''

Leo looked up and was about to thank her when Amanda came flying through the door.

''Oh, Daddy, we had such a wonderful time on the boat. You should have come. Mr. Eberhard even let me steer.'' Constance came in behind her, a thin, blond-haired girl wearing a Laura Ashley dress.

''Didn't we ever. Such fun. Amanda, you must tell your

father to get a boat so we can raft up and have picnics together.''

Amanda looked at her father and took his hand.

"Can we, Daddy?"

He stood up slowly. "Maybe, sweetheart. Come on, Mr. Barzeny's waiting in the car.'' He turned to the maid who looked like she wanted to disappear. "Thank you,'' he said to her in a tight voice, then walked toward the door.

Amanda gave Constance a little hug and followed her father out of the house. She noticed he was walking a little slower than usual, and his shoulders were kind of stooped, but she was so excited about her day that she let it pass. She was still bubbling over when she got to the car.

"Did you ever see such great sailing weather?'' she went on.

"You remember Mr. Barzeny from the time he came over for dinner, Amanda,'' Leo said. "We'll just drop him off back at the club.''

Amanda nodded and climbed into the back seat. Leo slid into the driver's seat, started the car, and pulled out.

"Have you ever been on a big sailboat, Mr. Barzeny?'' Amanda asked.

He chuckled. "I once made sailboat,'' he said, then added, "out of can of sardines. That's close as I came. It went twenty feet, then it sank.'' He turned around and gave her a big smile.

"Oh,'' she said, not knowing whether to smile with him or not. "We almost sank today also. It was so exciting.''

"Big boats like that don't sink, Amanda,'' her father said. "Unless they hit a rock.''

"Almost,'' she persisted. "When we first got out and the wind caught the sail we leaned way, way over. Felt like we were going to tip.''

"Probably just normal heeling,'' her father said and sped up as he turned onto the Boston Post Road.

"So how come Constance's mother started cursing and fiddling with the rope that pulls in the big sail? It was twisted or on wrong or something, and Mr. Eberhard was yelling at her the whole time. It was very exciting. Didn't you see it, Daddy? It was right at the beginning.''

"No honey, I didn't."

She sat back in the vinyl seat and nodded with conviction at Mr. Barzeny. "Took her ten minutes to get it back right. I don't suppose that's why your sardine can sank, was it?''

"No," the older Russian said with a grin. "Not enough ballast. I was hungry that day.''

Eighteen

THE NOTE READ:

Dear Harmon, I agree, Our Romance is a sure thing. I'm willing to take the kind of risk you suggested. Barbara.

The crumpled paper sat on Lieutenant Rucker's desk looking small and insignificant, but both men staring at it realized it was hot. Sergeant Nelson felt rightly proud to have hooked it in all his legwork, but he was even prouder of the scrap of information that came from Orantes, Perkins's section manager. The man was certain that Perkins was ambidextrous, having seen him both switch-hit and throw lefty and righty in the Rivetz summer softball league.

The biggest coup, however, came from Santini, much to Nelson's chagrin. After two days of checking out every small restaurant, lounge, and motel in lower Westchester, he had finally found a place where someone recognized the pictures of Barbara Perkins and Harmon Parrish. It was called the Acapulco Lounge and bore as much resemblance to the Mexican resort as near beer did to Napoleon brandy. But it was just the kind of place to which the two of them might go. Located over in the commercial district of White Plains, near the exit of the expressway, the lounge catered to long-haul truck drivers and short-haul women. The lights weren't dimmed, but they didn't have to be. No one was paying attention to anything except their own problems, which in most cases seemed to be how to eat, get laid, and make it back on the road in time for their next delivery. The bartender was polite when Santini showed him his badge and became downright friendly when he glanced at the pictures. He knew the situation had the markings of at least a ten spot, and maybe with a little luck, he could stretch it into a twenty. He artfully told Santini everything he could recall, which was just that they came in half a dozen times in the last six months, stayed for a sandwich and burger, maybe a beer or two, then left. Combined with the other pieces that were falling into place, Rucker figured he had enough to go to the assistant D.A. By noon he had an arrest warrant.

Nineteen

THEY BROUGHT LEO IN IN HANDCUFFS. Rucker made the collar in front of Leo's wife, child, and neighbors. The swirling red lights on the top of the patrol cars were beacons to the neighborhood, and by the time Leo was led out of his house, there were so many people on the street that it looked as if Gorbachev was about to pass. Few knew what the excitement was about, but they'd find out soon enough. Rucker had set up a news conference for 3:00 P.M.

that day, Sunday, in plenty of time to make the Monday-morning editions.

Leo Perkins was read his rights, booked, photographed, and tossed into a jail cell. The worst part of it all, the absolute horror that Leo couldn't forget, was the look on Amanda's face when they took him out the front door of his own house with his hands cuffed behind his back. The sons of bitches, he thought. They didn't have to do that. He'd have to live with that look for the rest of his life.

By four o'clock he found himself in a small cell with a bunch of Saturday-night rowdies and two liquor store stick-up artists. The room smelled, the men looked savage, and Leo felt an anger so fierce it was burning into his heart. But his cell mates left him alone because he was six foot three and his expression was so fierce, they feared that any provocation would cause him to explode. For the rest of the day, Leo sulked in the corner of the little cell by himself.

At five o'clock Leo's lawyer came to see him. He came straight out of the phone book under "Attorneys, criminal." His name was Sam Flagstaff and he looked neat and clean and very young. The first question was bail. Flagstaff asked how much money he could comfortably muster together. Without more than ten seconds' hesitation Leo mentioned a figure: "Ten thousand dollars, not including the Dodge Valiant."

"Not enough," Flagstaff said. "I think I can get the judge down to maybe fifty. Keep in mind it's a murder-two charge."

Leo felt like sinking through the floor. Fifty grand. Where the hell was he going to get that kind of money?

"I can get you a bond, but you got to put up the house."

"Already mortgaged . . . twice."

There was silence for a moment.

"You got a friend who could pledge his house? Wouldn't cost him anything unless you took a powder. Has to be unmortgaged though."

Leo grimaced. You went out to dinner with friends, watched baseball games and drank beer with friends. What you didn't do was ask them to pledge their houses to the tune of fifty thousand dollars.

"Maybe," he said finally. Reluctantly he wrote Hanley's and Sollie's names and addresses on a piece of paper and handed it to the young lawyer. Flagstaff put it in his pocket and told him he'd try his best.

"You got two things going for you," he said, pushing back from the cell. "It's your first arrest."

"Yeah, and what's the other?" Leo asked skeptically.

"Me," Flagstaff said with a grin. "I'm great on criminal cases."

"I thought that's all you did," Leo said.

"Mostly," the lawyer answered. "Plus a little negligence and estates. I'm flexible," he added. "You'll see."

Twenty

THE GOOD NEWS WAS THAT BAIL WAS GO-ing to be set at fifty thousand dollars, the bad news was that neither Hanley nor Sollie was able to come up with either the money or a way to guarantee it. That left Leo in the small cell, wondering what in hell to do next. Barbara had been allowed to visit once, and the two of them had talked about their possibilities. Maybe they could piece it together, a home equity loan, extend the limit on the Master Charge, maybe Barbara's brother in Ohio was good for five thousand. But it all would take time, up to a week even, and a week in the degrading jail was too painful to think about. The Saturday-night rowdies were already out, replaced by a young man with enough needle holes in his arm to pass for a sponge. A week in there was impossible. And Amanda needed him around, explaining things from his side, not visiting her father in a jail cell.

So, Leo thought, it's finally come home. You live in the expensive New York suburbs on the edge of your income and there's no room for play, no cushion for emergencies. You think you got it all covered with health insurance, extended appliance warranties, the Christmas clubs, and something comes along and flattens you. Maybe that's what friends were for, in which case he certainly had chosen wrong. He knew Sollie had a gun collection worth easily twenty thousand dollars he could pledge, and Hanley had bragged about working his mortgage off, something you could do if your kid didn't take piano lessons. Some friends, good for a lunch break and a few beers after work, and no more. That hurt him. He turned away from the bars and slumped down to the floor.

He didn't come out of his black mood even when his name was called by the guard two hours later. It was 8:00 P.M. and Leo thought he was being given his dinner. He expected to see a tin plate of food being shoved at him, but instead he saw the jailer unlock the door and motion him outside.

"You've been released," the officer said. "Guy is outside who put up the bail."

How the hell did Flagstaff do that? Leo thought with surprise and got up quickly. Maybe Sollie had second thoughts about his collection . . .

But the friendly face that greeted him when he emerged into the clerk's office for his release papers wasn't Flagstaff's or Hanley's or Sollie's. It belonged to a little man with a big forehead and a sharp pointed chin, one Jakob Barzeny, the wizard of McArdle's chess club.

"So," Jakob smiled, "they took good long time."

"But how . . . ?"

"Come," the older man said. "I explain. But first some chicken soup. I think a lot better on full stomach."

Twenty-one

"IN RUSSIA I WAS POLICEMAN," BARZENY said over the steaming bowl of soup. "A Jewish policeman in Khrushchev's Russia, but there are many contradictions in my country. I lived in little city called Volkhov on Lake Ladoga not far from Leningrad. A pretty town, but even pretty little towns have drunks and robbers and murderers." He ladled a spoon of the hot liquid into his mouth, and Leo watched as the older man smiled in appreciation. He took another sip and went on. "I was smartest boy in my school except," he shrugged, "I was hopeless romantic. When it comes time for me to get job I think what could be better than being policeman and upholding the laws of our progressive society? At the time did I realize that half of party regulars were involved in *chornirynok*, the black market, and other shady dealings? Idealism lasted three years and for ten years longer momentum carried me. First I walked streets, then I become investigator. But by then I was doing an empty job. Along the way I find chess and the game becomes for me reason to live. I am grand master at thirty-three and can think of nothing else."

"I thought you came from Moscow," Leo said.

"I moved." Barzeny bent down closer to the bowl and drank some more soup. "I moved because I got invitation to come and teach at Moscow Chess Academy. I left Volkhov and its crooks and entered world of politics." He smiled. "In Russia, nothing is so political as chess." He raised a bony finger. "This was in fifties and early sixties, and a Jew

71

like Kasparov had not yet made spotlight. I was first,'' he said, "but problem is I am not quite good enough.'' He brought his two bony fingers almost together. "I was that far away. Far enough to keep me from international tournaments. A Jew, representing Mother Russia?'' He shook his head. "So in '65 I make plan. I do three things. First thing is I look around for young man to coach, but young man with future. I know I never will be allowed to leave Russia as player, but as coach is possible. And I find Grigory Ivorenko who thinks I am God. This is not quite so, but I can teach him how to win, and best of all, Ivorenko has father who is big admiral in Baltic Fleet. By '69 I am traveling to Europe twice a year.'' Barzeny took another spoonful of soup and wiped his mouth with a napkin.

"Second thing I do is start playing in private for money. In Russia this goes very slowly, but always you can find someone to gamble a ruble or two on a game. With luck, you find someone with bigger pocketbook. After several years I have saved up over four thousand rubles when I hear of a man called Viktor Metropian.''

Leo leaned forward. "Jakob, this is all very interesting, but I don't see where this explains how you managed to bail me out of jail.''

"Patience, I keep telling you Leo, is your biggest problem. Longer your pieces remain on board, more possibilities appear.'' He patted Leo's hand. "This Metropian,'' he continued, "is as rich as Greek ship owner, black market or something. His Achilles heel is chess. This I find out when he starts coming to academy looking to get into games . . . for big money. No one wants to play because he is good enough to make draw. Under pressure of losing several hundred rubles a game, even steadiest players make mistakes. But not me. I arranged to play him for four thousand rubles each game.'' Barzeny smiled in remembering. "This was fabulous sum of money. If I lost first game it would have been end for me, but fortunately I beat him on passed pawn threat and offsides knight fork. For the next ten hours we played, and at end I had his wallet and forty thousand rubles. It was to him pleasant although costly diversion. For me it was freedom." Barzeny tipped the soup bowl and caught the last remaining drop of liquid in his spoon. He sat back with a contented smile on his face before continuing. Finally he spoke.

"The third thing I do takes another three years, '73 to '76. The money I keep hidden away, but twice a year I travel back to Volkhov and my friends from police days, all with interesting contacts. I am soon introduced to Leningrad stamp dealer, man with both knowledge and discretion. This second is the most important. In six trips I buy six stamps, slowly. By November '76 I am ready."

"And the money?" Leo asked.

"All in the stamps, except four thousand I take with me to an international match in Vienna. Ivorenko does very well until the day I defect. Then I hear he loses all his matches afterwards. No one there to hold his hand."

"Vienna?" Leo asked.

"Then on to New York. Always I hear about New York. Place of great opportunity, place of Bobby Fischer. But I get horrible rate on the four thousand rubles and am forced to sell one stamp. I arrive in your country and find enough things to do to keep me from selling other stamps. Then in 1983 I get sick and this causes me to cash in another. Medicine in your country . . ." he shook his head. "Anyway, from this little stamp I have been living." He looked carefully into Leo's eyes. "I am used to living simply. The four other stamps I keep in small hidden box, mementos of my homeland. They're all from czarist Russia and one even is from time of Nicholas the First. But in their dark little box they were silently growing . . . how you say it, appreciating, and when I bring them in this afternoon for appraisal, I almost do not believe it what I am hearing, they are now worth over sixty thousand dollars."

Leo's eyes opened wide. "You pledged a stamp collection worth sixty thousand dollars to get me out of jail?" He looked at him skeptically.

"I did," he nodded. "Because after playing chess with a man you know him, sometimes better than he knows himself. I knew Victor Metropian was gambler at heart and would damage his positions by taking foolish chances, chances I was pleased to offer. I knew that before I sit down with him and this is how I beat him. I know you, Leo, never back away from confrontation and have a strong sense of honor . . . even in defeat. My stamps are safe with bondsman, I have no worry of that.''

"I am amazed," Leo said simply. "And not quite sure why you did it in any case."

"Because I know also police have made mistake. There is no way you could kill anyone, Leo, you not crazy or ruthless enough. But," he smiled, "you do like good fight and so I give you opportunity to get your pieces on the board. The game's already in progress and now you're out, and it is your move."

"Thanks," Leo said. He sat in silence for a moment. Finally he looked up. "I could use some help."

Barzeny smiled and pushed back from the table. "It would be great honor," he said. "But now I think your family is waiting. Perhaps we meet tomorrow evening at McArdle's?''

Leo stood up and shook his hand. Then he put on his coat and turned toward the door.

"You are forgetting something," Barzeny said and held up the check for the bowl of soup. "You always pay, remember?''

Twenty-two

HE WAS AFRAID TO ASK HER. THAT NIGHT, after Amanda had cried herself to sleep and they were sitting at the kitchen table, he thought it would be easy, but he must have started half a dozen times and retreated. What was he going to say, especially since she'd spent the last hour comforting him? "Hey, honey, were you and Parrish screwing each other? Am I going to wind up in jail for the rest of my life because you were balling some son-of-a-bitch music teacher and were too chicken to tell me?" How the hell do you begin a conversation like that? But it had to be done. He couldn't overlook the note Eberhard's maid had found.

"Barbara," Leo finally began. "Lieutenant Rucker's going to ask you a lot of questions . . . none of which you have to answer."

"There's nothing to tell him anyway," she said. "It's obviously some big, stupid mistake."

"But there is something," Leo continued, "that I'd like you to tell me. I'm going to ask you once, and whatever you say, I'll believe you. I don't think you've ever lied to me."

"I never have," she said, looking at him now with a frown.

Leo hesitated. It was true, she had never lied to him. That was one thing he had always counted on in their years together. But then again, maybe she had been only laying the groundwork for that once-in-a-lifetime whopper. Who the hell knew? Or maybe she had lied and he just had never caught her.

"Were you and Harmon Parrish having an affair?" he asked. He wanted to look away, but there was something so deadly about the question he was compelled to see its effect on her. He wasn't prepared for her response.

"An affair?" She stubbed out the cigarette she was smoking. "With Harmon!" She laughed. It was tight laughter but it was genuine, the kind of laugh she might have given if he had asked her in all seriousness if her mother had been a snake charmer with the Hungarian State Circus. He looked at her amused features, her now-rounded doe eyes, and her full mouth pulled into the beginning of a grin, but he still couldn't see the joke. What he saw instead with poignancy was the beautiful woman he had married fifteen years earlier. Before Amanda and before the house with the two mortgages in Harrison. Barbara shook her head through the swirling smoke.

"No, Leo. Never. How could you think . . ."

"There was a note," he interrupted, "that Harmon must have dropped at the Eberhards' after leaving here . . . signed Barbara."

"That said . . . ?" She looked puzzled.

"Something about your romance being risky. I didn't see the note or the signature. It could be nothing." He shrugged but she could tell that the note was vital to him.

A light appeared in her eyes, but then just as suddenly a curtain closed over it. She leaned back and took a deep breath. "An affair with the music teacher?" She shook her head. "Never. He was an entertaining man and sometimes he came early and we chatted." She hesitated. "I suppose I've written him notes from time to time about scheduling Amanda's lessons or some other thing . . . but sleep with him?" She reached out for Leo's hand. "I wouldn't do that to you, Leo."

He looked down at her hand in his and after a moment gave it a little squeeze. "He's going to ask, that's all," Leo said. "Rucker is. That's what he's working up. My killing Parrish out of jealousy. I wanted you to be clear about it."

"He's crazy," she said forcibly. "And I'll tell him."

Of course she would, Leo thought. But would it be good enough?

Twenty-three

THE OFFICES OF THE ADVANCED ANSWER-ing Services Company were located in a building that had started out life as an undistinguished one-floor frame house wedged in between a brick storefront and the Harrison fire-department maintenance yard. It had since lost its interior walls and, except for the single bathroom, was now one open space with several half-wall cubicles. The largest one was in a far corner and served as the main office of the company. Inside it were several file cabinets and a typewriter sitting on top of a metal desk. The other cubicles had desks, on each of which was a telephone with numbered buttons referenced to a card Scotch-taped to the desk top indicating which client was being called. This, plus a Mr. Coffee machine on the entry table, was the sum total of the Advanced Answering Service Company. At 1:00 A.M. that night, the place was deserted, since live operator service went from eight in the morning until midnight. The door was locked but since there was little of value to steal, there were no burglar alarms, and some of the windows were still open. It was through one of these windows that the lone figure stole into the building.

The thin beam of light stabbed into the darkness and played over the entire open space before settling down to the telephones on the desk tops and their referenced cards. One by one the telephone numbers next to the phones were inspected until one was selected in the third cubicle. The intruder sat down at the desk and opened the drawer underneath. The light flashed inside and illuminated a bunch of pencils, a small sharpener, some thumb tacks, and a large spiral notebook. The person reached in, withdrew the notebook, and started reading through the pages. Each one was dated and had several entries. First one, then another of the pages was ripped out and stuffed into the intruder's pocket. Then the book was closed and put back in the drawer. The telephone on the desk suddenly began ringing, and the intruder froze while closing the drawer. The light was snapped off and darkness closed in again on the small office. After a few seconds the phone stopped ringing, and shortly thereafter the person stood up and crept back to the open window. In less than a minute the figure had disappeared.

Twenty-four

IF ORANTES HAD HAD AN OFFICE HE would have surrounded Leo with the trappings of his authority before delivering the message. As it was, he called him over behind the mirrored-back china hutch with carved pediment top and Goddard-style block-front, three-drawer buffet base to inform him he was being reassigned.

"What?" Leo couldn't believe his ears.

"In view of what they saw on television last night, they thought it best if you were less public. Being a salesman is kind of like being an ambassador for Rivetz . . ." Orantes fumbled. "The publicity people figured maybe it would be better for the store if you weren't so visible."

"What does that mean?" Leo asked angrily. "You want me to wear a mask?" But he knew what was coming.

"Not me, actually," Orantes said. "It was their idea. I just kind of . . . agreed."

"I'll bet."

"Only temporarily, you understand, until this thing blows over. We got a slot for you out back in the warehouse, something like inventory control."

"And lose my commissions . . ."

Orantes looked at him closely. "Considering the fact you were never one of our best floormen, I think you'll still make out." Orantes did his best to keep from smiling. "It's either that or finding a position elsewhere."

"You make the six o'clock news and wind up losing your job. What kind of shit is that? And after ten years."

78

"Not lost, Perkins, reassigned. You can understand. Rivetz has always been loyal to its employees, but on the other hand it does not want to present a . . ." he searched for the right word, "a negative image to the public."

"Negative? I know more about dining room tables than I do about inventory control." Leo was feeling a tightness in his collar. "I know enough not to buy a goddamn slab of marble that's never going to sell. Talk about negative . . ."

"Shouting won't do you any good, Perkins. Besides, it's only temporary. Hey, you might be back in my department in a few months." Orantes's smile finally broke through. "You got to believe I did my best."

"Fuck you," Leo said and moved past him. As he did he shoved him a little out of the way.

"They're expecting you out back," Orantes snarled. "If you're not there by ten you can kiss your pension good-bye. You ask me, you're lucky you still got a job, whether or not you killed that guy."

Perkins went over to his desk and retrieved his sales book. In one swift motion, he hurled the thick book up and out over the dining room sales floor. Loose order forms fluttered down like confetti over the inventory of mahogany tables before the heavy leather binder shattered a Japanese Midori vase as it dropped for a landing.

"I'm going," Leo said in the direction of the section manager and turned to walk out. Twenty yards away he passed through the lighting section, where he saw Hanley watching him and looking very uncomfortable.

"Yeah, and fuck you too as well as Sollie, my two best friends," he said without breaking stride. He didn't even look back. He walked straight into Patio Furniture and made a right turn in the direction of the warehouse.

Part of every good salesman's job is to know the inventory. Leo was no stranger to the warehouse. He knew where just about everything was located, and he knew many of the fork-truck operators. That didn't mean he felt comfortable in the cavernous space or happy with his new job title. The warehouse men were known as "inventory jockeys" and had the thankless job of counting stock and checking that everything was where it was supposed to be. A flat salary to match a flat, boring job. Between the four trailerloads a day that came into the warehouse and the dozen or so outgoing delivery trucks, not to mention the scores of private cars picking up merchandise, the opportunities for theft were numerous. But the inventory jocks, and there were three of them, just counted and marked locations. That was their contribution. Occasionally something mildly interesting came up, like sighting a heretofore missing item, but for the most part the job was a lot of walking, a lot of climbing, and a lot of complaining. There was nothing less than a city of furniture waiting to be counted and recounted.

Leo reported to the manager's booth near the front loading dock and was given an inventory clipboard. Peterson, the man in charge, was either unaware of Leo's celebrity or playing a role worthy of an Oscar. The two men knew each other casually, but Peterson didn't say a word about Leo's problems. He told a few jokes, ran through the drill of Leo's new job, told a few more jokes, introduced Perkins to the other men, then looked at his watch and told him to be back by twelve-thirty, lunchtime.

"It's kind of overwhelming at first, but you'll get used to it in a few days," Peterson said. "But I still don't understand why you came out here from the sales floor. Most of the guys out here want to get in."

Leo cracked a smile. "I figured I could use the exercise," he said. "It's about time I got off my ass."

Twenty-five

EVEN IN THE GIGANTIC WAREHOUSE, THE immense slab of marble was hard to conceal. There it sat, on its equally imposing marble legs, in aisle O, right next to the main center artery. It dwarfed all the other marble objects around it in that section known to the salesmen as the quarry. In aisle O alone there was enough marble to redesign the Baths of Caracalla. The edge of Orantes's two-inch-thick marble table was protected by a thick insulating cushion, while only a thin layer of cardboard protected the legs. Leo figured all it would take was a regular packing timber wedged between one of the legs and the outside frame of the cubbyhole. Then a solid bump from one of the lift trucks as it turned into the main aisle and with any luck, a chunk of the leg would pop off. Leo rationalized that he was doing it for his co-workers in Dining Rooms to keep the marble leviathan from eating their commissions, but in his heart he knew it was nothing more than a shameless act of revenge. Revenge for the spineless treatment from Orantes and his superiors, and revenge for the web of circumstances that had turned him into a murder defendant out on bail. His pent-up anger had found a victim, even if it was only an innocent, overworked piece of stone. In ten minutes he had the whole thing rigged. The fork trucks were always sideswiping the end metal cubbies, but just to help matters he put a full open container of coffee on the floor on the opposite side of the aisle. That would steer the drivers over to the table's side.

Then he went off, clipboard in hand, to do an honest day's work.

Twenty-six

MCARDLE'S WAS BUSY THAT EVENING. FOR the small chess club that meant four tables going, with a handful of kibitzers looking on. From the glances he got as he entered, people looking up from their board positions and wasting precious seconds of their clock to watch him, Leo understood that McArdle's had heard of his problems. But no one came over as Leo moved over toward Barzeny. He was in a corner by himself analyzing a position on one of the two empty tables. A cold cup of coffee was by his elbow and his eyes, focusing on the pieces before him, looked like lasers. "Mate in three," Jakob said without raising his head. "Black to move."

Leo sat down opposite him and took a moment to study the pieces. Black was hopelessly out of position.

"Impossible," he said.

"Ah, but not with queen sacrifice." Barzeny moved the black queen to F2 and had it taken by the white knight. "Unexpected, yes, but see how it opens door for rook." He brought the black rook into a fork and immediately Leo saw the mating move with his queen's bishop's pawn.

Leo sat back. "One doesn't usually sacrifice a queen in the end game."

"Sometimes," Barzeny answered, "one has to gamble everything." He looked up to the younger man's eyes. "And how are you feeling tonight?"

"I could be better. Seems with my friends and employer, you're guilty until proven innocent."

"I am sorry, Leo. But now is no time for remorse. We must calculate our next move. Even now, the forces that oppose you are building case. So we have to build ours." Barzeny took a sip of the cold coffee and made a face. He took another swallow and reached into his right side pocket. When his hand came out it held a bunch of pistachio nuts. He cracked one, put it in his mouth, and put the shells into his left side pocket. Barzeny's nut addiction was legendary in the club. More than once his opponents complained that he used the noise of the cracking shells to disrupt their thought.

"Only way I can help you," he said, "is to approach it like chess game. The first question, what is opponent like?"

"Lieutenant Rucker?"

"No, real opponent is murderer. He's one moving the pieces. Rucker is just one of them. How do we find out about murderer? By finding out about Parrish." He tossed another pistachio nut into his mouth and again placed the two empty shells into the pocket on the other side. "Parrish will lead you to murderer."

"But Parrish is dead."

"Yes, is true, but what do you know about him?"

Leo placed his hand palm upward. "A local piano teacher. I suppose he has a bunch of references."

"And how you say . . . gossip?" Barzeny asked. "Anything unusual?"

Leo thought for a long moment. At one of the nearby tables a king had just been checkmated, and the onlookers started an immediate and loud postmortem. As was the norm, everyone but the defeated player had a dozen ways to have escaped.

"I asked Amanda what he was like, and she said something funny this morning," Leo began. "Apparently Parrish would disappear for a few minutes during the end of the lesson while the students practiced alone. He called it 'independent summary' or something like that. It was a time for the students to take a breath, get their heads together, and bring the day's lesson into focus. So he'd leave the room for seven or eight minutes, then come back, and they'd perform one final time for him. Sort of like a mini-concert.'' Barzeny raised his eyes. "What I think now," Leo continued, "is that Parrish used the time to roam through the houses and rob them. I conducted my own little survey when a pair of my cuff links turned up missing, and I found four houses where something was stolen. That's only his Tuesday lessons.'' He let that sink in for a minute. "Amanda had another story about him, too. Last week, one of the other girls in Amanda's class at school, Meredith Thorson, who also took piano with Parrish, got tired of waiting and went looking for her teacher. She found him in the butler's pantry arguing with the family maid. They clammed up when she poked her head in, but not before Meredith caught something about the maid owing Parrish some money."

Barzeny leaned back. "For what?"

"Didn't say. Maybe he did an errand for her or brought her something. Some of the maids in those big houses are very isolated. If they get out one day a week, that's a lot."

"So," Barzeny said, "first thing to find out is why woman owes him money. Then to find out is what other things Parrish was doing during his 'independent summaries.' "

Leo nodded. "I could try that."

"What puzzles me," Barzeny continued, "is why murderer chose such strange way to kill. I read where it was piano string. Ask yourself, Leo, would you use such a method to kill someone? Wouldn't gun or knife be simpler?"

"Availability. Maybe the killer didn't come with killing in mind. He just improvised when he got there."

"No, Leo, from description, garrote was obviously made before. If it was unexpected murder, such a weapon is the last object that would be used. This is important. If there was one thing I learned as policeman, is there is reason for everything. I want us to look at it."

"I'll ask Flagstaff," Leo said.

"And ask him for names also," Barzeny said. "Who are police using in their case, who discovered body, who were friends? We cannot begin strategy without more information." He shook his head and reached into his pocket for another handful of pistachio nuts. "It's like playing without material. At present moment your king is alone and defenseless on the board." He picked all the pieces off the board in front of him except the black king. Then he cracked two more nuts and offered one to Leo.

"No, thank you."

"Perhaps not all alone," he continued. "I think I can place another piece on your side of board."

"And how is that?"

Barzeny crunched down on the nuts and motioned with his head surreptitiously. "The man in vest who just lost game is Doctor Ingrahm, county medical examiner. We have played several games together. He comes usually on Monday evenings. Have you never played with him, Leo?"

Leo leaned a little to the right to get a better look. "No, I'm not usually here on Monday."

"Well, I hope to get with him into a game later this evening," Barzeny said. "He does not have to know I help you. This is little piece of luck we cannot overlook. Maybe I will let him beat me one time . . ."

"Now, that is a sacrifice," Leo said.

"I find," Barzeny said, "that when someone is lucky to win game from me, they become light in head." He leaned forward and lowered his voice. "I know in Russia, often there were things police kept to themselves, details very helpful had defense learned of them early enough." He sat back. "If you would be good enough to now make yourself go away, I will proceed. We can meet again tomorrow night."

Twenty-seven

GETTING THE NAME OF THE THORSON maid was simpler than Leo expected. That night Amanda simply called her friend and hung up an hour later with the information. Along the way the two adolescents had touched upon the nerdiness of just about every boy in the class, the economic profile of most of the girls as discerned by a dissection of their wardrobes, and the small peculiarities of domestic help. Amanda was winging the last subject, since the closest she had ever come to such a luxury was when the Durabrite man had come to clean the living room rug three months earlier. In any case, she found out that Meredith's maid's name was Hilda Gruner and that she had been with them for almost a year, long enough to lose her immigrant innocence but not her Berlin accent. She was twenty and was hoping to save enough money to enroll in a New York art school, although she hadn't yet confided that to Mr. or Mrs. Thorson.

The next morning at precisely eight forty-five Leo was waiting outside the Thorson house. In an effort to alter his looks, his hair was slicked back, and he was wearing a heavy-framed pair of nonprescription reading glasses with a light smoky tint, purchased at a nearby drugstore. He had watched Meredith leave on the school bus at eight-thirty, and her father in his Mercedes a few minutes later.

The woman who answered the door had a twenty-year-old's complexion but an expression that reminded Leo of Marlene Dietrich in *Blue Angel*. The gray-and-white maid's uniform she wore was decidedly snug around her hips. She looked Leo over and decided that a six-foot-three man in a suit and tie should be given an opportunity to speak, but not necessarily shown any hospitality.

"Are you Hilda Gruner?" Leo asked.

The young woman's eyes opened wide. She thought that the only people who knew her full name were the Thorsons and the mailman, and by no stretch of the imagination was this man from the post office.

"Yes," she said. "I am Hildegarde."

"May I come in?" Leo asked politely. "I'm from the Department of Immigration." He reached in his pocket and flashed a badge. Had she studied it closely she would have noticed it had been issued by the Harrison Volunteer School Crossing Guards Association, which Barbara had been a member of when Amanda was in third grade. Fortunately his announcement stunned her and she didn't move for a moment. Leo waited, and finally she stepped back.

"Mrs. Thorson is not at home?" Leo asked.

"She is asleep, but we can go into the kitchen," she said nervously. She turned and Leo followed her down a hallway and through a dining room that looked like it could seat two dozen people comfortably. The kitchen they entered appeared equal to the task of feeding them.

Hilda spoke first in a tight, controlled voice.

"What do you want?"

Leo looked around slowly, then sat down.

"I need some information," he said. "This does not concern the fact that your visitor's visa has expired and you are here illegally now," he said, smiling. "But it might." He waited a moment. "If you are cooperative I am sure our department can temporarily overlook your tardiness in leaving the country. My interest is not with you, Miss Gruner, but with Harmon Parrish."

The young woman visibly stiffened. She turned, opened a drawer under one of the granite counter tops, and withdrew a pack of cigarettes. She lit one nervously, then came over and sat down next to Leo.

"Mr. Parrish?" She frowned.

"Yes, you remember. He came here once a week," Leo said pointedly. "The police department has reason to believe that he was involved in some shady dealings and has asked us to help."

"I thought they already arrested someone," Hilda said quickly and took a puff of her cigarette. "It was in the paper."

Leo leaned forward and tried to maintain his stern expression. If he was going out on a limb, now was the time. He cleared his throat. "Information has come in, Miss Gruner, that in some of the houses where he gave lessons, Parrish was in the habit of demanding money from some of the domestic help who, like yourself, were here illegally. The police department has asked us to check on this because it's possible that one of the people being blackmailed killed Parrish." He sat back but kept his eyes on her face. "Was Parrish extorting money from you?"

She took another puff, then bit her lip. Her eyes met his and stayed there for a moment.

"No," she said finally. "He tried. Six months ago he demanded money, but I told him I'd tell Mr. Thorson, who is a lawyer, and have him thrown in jail."

Bingo, Leo thought. "And you expect me to believe he accepted that?"

Hilda looked down at the tabletop and nodded. "I never paid him any money for blackmail. He was an evil man and I didn't want any part of him. I told you, he tried but I resisted."

Leo shook his head slowly. "I don't know what to think, Miss Gruner, because I have a problem with that."

Her eyes flashed back up at him. "Why is that?"

"Because Parrish left a little black notebook with names and amounts of money owed to him. That is why I am here. Your name is on page eight, and you're down for a considerable sum." He watched while that sunk in. She tried to hold her defiant expression, but the edges of her mouth started to drop. "I told you in the beginning if you were truthful we would cooperate. I am sure you don't want to become a suspect in this investigation. I'll ask you again, was he blackmailing you and did he ever mention anyone else he was blackmailing?''

She took a last deep puff of her cigarette and crushed it out. A grandfather clock somewhere inside the house rang out the fact that it was nine o'clock, but it had no effect on either of them.

"It wasn't for blackmail," she said finally. "It was for drugs."

Leo sat back. Blindsided by the obvious. Drugs, drugs, goddamn drugs everywhere. And Parrish was dealing them to the housebound maids if he couldn't scare them with exposure. Very pretty.

"Marijuana, sometimes hashish," Hilda continued. "Nothing heavy." She leaned forward. "Sometimes it gets so lonely here, there's only Meredith to talk to and she's twelve. Smoking was the only way to forget where I was, what I was doing. Back in Germany I would have laughed if you told me I'd wind up as a housemaid. But that was the only job I could find and still stay here in America." She started to laugh but Leo figured it was only to cover up the moisture that was in her eyes.

"He was a bum, Mr. Parrish was, a real bum. A week behind in your payment and he'd have a fit. Next time the stuff would be so cut it would take a whole ounce just to get high. Then every now and then he'd get the urge to pocket a little something extra from the Thorsons' bedroom and ask me to tell him what wouldn't be missed. But I refused. I didn't want to help him steal.''

"Did he ever mention anyone else who he was supplying? Or extorting?''

She shook her head. "I think there were others, but I never found out who. He provided a service that was hard to pass up. Home delivery. I'm sure there were plenty. He always told me I was the only one to complain about the quality of the stuff he was giving. But we never spent a lot of time talking because he'd have to hurry back to Meredith's lesson.'' She dried her eyes. "It was a laugh, it really was. And here the whole time the Thorsons thought they had a saint teaching their daughter.'' A thought struck her and her face took on a confused look. "But if you have his book, you should be able to find the others."

Leo stood up. "We are following that up. I thought you might have some personal knowledge."

She shook her head. "So how long do I have left before I have to leave the country?" she asked resignedly. "I should give the Thorsons some notice."

"No need," Leo said airily as he walked to the front of the house. "You cooperate with us, we cooperate with you. I'll let myself out." He opened the front door and passed through, leaving her standing in the kitchen like a statue.

Twenty-eight

LEO MADE IT TO WORK BY NINE-THIRTY and saw, to his dismay, that the marble table was still intact. The night watchman had taken the full coffee cup away so Leo replaced it with a light bulb. He knew the lift-truck operators would be too lazy to get down from their trucks to pick it up and walk twenty feet with it to the waste basket. They'd just avoid hitting it and maybe clip the side of the steel enclosure. Bye-bye table leg.

By eleven-thirty Leo was over in aisle B7 counting boxes of 36-by-48-inch abstract paintings from some guy in New Jersey who shipped in two dozen a week. Each one was a slight variation on what looked like the same theme, the collision of three planets in a bowl of noodle soup. Leo himself had sold five of the works which, strangely enough, went well with the Futura dining room ensemble. Peterson walked over to him and announced that he had an outside phone call.

"Some guy by the name of Flagstaff. Extension eight." Leo nodded and took the call on the telephone in the main aisle.

"Sorry to get you at work, Leo, but I wanted to keep you aware of what's going on. The D.A. is going for the indictment next week to the grand jury so we'll know a little of their case by then. They'll be holding some stuff back, but by the deposition we'll have all the names of their witnesses and a clear picture of what we'll be up against. In the meantime we get a chance to beat the bushes for ourselves. Let me tell you what I've got so far. I have a friend who works as a police clerk and occasionally peeks into their computer records. I persuaded her to do just that on Mr. Harmon Parrish and guess what came back?"

"Parrish was once arrested on a minor drug charge," Leo answered.

There was silence on the other end of the line.

"How'd you know?"

"I'm way ahead of you. I met one of his customers, a maid at one of the houses where he taught." Leo watched as a fork truck passed him and headed up the center aisle. It swerved two feet to the right when it passed the light bulb but missed the metal cage by a good ten inches. Leo shook his head, then spoke into the phone. "Parrish was also into extortion, thievery, and God knows what else. It's amazing who rich people allow past their big-bucks security systems these days. Stone fences to the world at large and open doors to all sorts of con artists."

Flagstaff grunted. "I'll need all the details, Leo. The more layers we can peel away from Parrish's veneer, the better for your case. You have to help me."

"You have to help me too," Leo said. "I want to see the murder weapon. Can you arrange it?"

"Sure. We're allowed." There was a pause on the line. "How's your wife holding up?"

"Under the circumstances, pretty good. If looks could kill, the town of Harrison would have murdered her already. Even the checkout girls at the supermarket have found her guilty. All talk ceases when she's in line."

"That'll all change when the grand jury doesn't indict you."

"You mean, 'if' it doesn't," Leo replied. He watched as another lift truck swerved and barely brushed by the cubicle. "I'm going to get you more information," Leo continued. "There's another maid who I can talk to about Parrish. I need some confirmation on the extortion part."

"Come in tomorrow after work," Flagstaff said. "And Leo, be careful. The murderer is still out there."

"Hell, I'm his meal ticket. I'm probably the last person he'd want to eliminate. See you tomorrow." Leo hung up the phone and walked back to the bin of abstract paintings to continue the count. He didn't hurry. After that stack there was another one of pastel beachscapes, and then another of still lifes with waterfowl. Today was art appreciation day, he figured. Why rush it?

Twenty-nine

NEXT ON THE LIST WAS THERESA, THE EBER-hards' maid, the young girl who had spoken to him about the note. Amanda had also supplied her name. Leo made the call during his lunch break, hoping that he'd be lucky and she'd answer, but the voice that came down the line had the measured assurance of employer, not employee.

"Hello, this is Pilar."

Leo was prepared. "I'm sorry to trouble you," he said, putting a little more nose into the words. "I'm calling for Theresa Mullins. This is Martin Philipps calling, one of the assistant registrars at Westchester Community College."

There was a hesitation for a moment, then Mrs. Eberhard spoke again. "Mr. Phillips, Theresa is no longer working with us. She left yesterday, quite unexpectedly. She decided to go back home to Ireland. I can give you an address."

"To Ireland," Leo repeated. "That's strange. She inquired by mail only one week ago about our evening programs in Fashion and Merchandising. There are some places open in our Tuesday evening class. That's what I was calling her about. You're sure?"

"Positive. She got a phone call two days ago and just packed up that night. We were very annoyed because she didn't even give us two weeks' notice to find a replacement. She said there was some trouble at home." Mrs. Eberhard took a breath, then said, "I wasn't aware that she was interested in night school."

Leo rumpled some papers, then said, "Yes, last week we got her note. Here it is, asking about some of our courses from our bulletin. Perhaps if you gave me that address I could just send her the information."

"In Ireland?"

"I'm just doing my job, madam. Maybe she'll return soon."

There was a delay, then finally Mrs. Eberhard spoke. "It's funny, Mr. Phillips, you sound familiar."

"Perhaps, people have been accusing me of sounding like Johnny Cash for years."

"No, someone else . . . I can't quite place it."

"You have that address?" Leo asked.

"Just a minute," she answered and put the phone down. In a minute she was back. "Theresa Mullins, 43 Gwathmey Terrace, Macroom, County Cork, Ireland. I think that's it."

"Thank you," Leo said and hung up. Now what the hell was this, he thought, looking at the paper in his hand. He didn't believe in coincidences, and this one was about the rankest he had come across in years. The girl leaves the country a few days before he has a chance to question her? He looked at his watch, added the six-hour time difference, and decided to go ahead and follow it up. He used his calling-card number, and with some help he had the Cork telephone information operator in less than two minutes.

"In Macroom," Leo said. "Mullins at 43 Gwathmey Terrace."

He waited, listening, while more than three thousand miles away a young woman pressed some keys on a computer.

"I don't have a Mullins listed at that address."

"Do you have any Mullinses on Gwathmey Terrace?" Leo asked.

"About fifteen," she answered, "but none at number 43. Then again, they may not have a telephone." She waited politely for a few seconds. "Is there anything else . . . ?"

"No, thank you," Leo said and hung up. Getting hold of little Theresa was not going to be so easy. Best thing would be to drop her a note and ask her to call . . . collect. Hell, calling up fifteen families with the name Mullins long distance was insane. As insane as a young maid leaving town the day before Leo wanted to talk to her. My luck, Leo thought, had better start changing soon. Real soon.

Thirty

BARZENY PUT ON HIS BEST CLOTHES, THE rust-colored suit and a slightly frayed white shirt, and went out calling. He took the bus to Yonkers and after some effort, found number 56 Sylvan Avenue. Yonkers was a mystery to him. A city large enough to be a major urban center in Russia, but in America only a poor stepchild to the likes of neighboring New York City. But Yonkers had some attractive lower-middle-class neighborhoods, and Sylvan Avenue was one of them. A row of well-tended houses with flowered window boxes ran along the curving street, garbage cans were neatly arranged at the curb, and brick side alleys were strangely devoid of graffiti. Number 56 was a four-story brownstone that had been converted into a multiple residence. If the intercom in the front could be trusted, Blanka Sologyar lived on the second floor in 2B. Barzeny pushed the buzzer and waited.

"Who is it?" he heard a woman say.

"It's Mr. Barzeny. I called you earlier." He stood back and in a moment there was a loud noise as the front door was electrically released. He climbed the staircase to the second floor slowly, wondering just how to handle this interview. He was there under false pretenses, so he had to find a way to get her, as they say in Russia, to chirp a little. On the phone he had spoken to her only about his association with The Eastern European Emigré League, but now he had to make his story plausible enough for her to talk openly with him. After straightening the cap on his head, he pushed her buzzer. The door opened just wide enough to stop on the chain, and he saw behind it the puzzled expression of a woman in her late fifties.

"Mrs. Sologyar," Barzeny said. "Very kind to see me. I can come in?"

She eyed him closely, squinted once, then opened the door.

"Excuse the mess," she said. "I wasn't really expecting anyone. You said you were with the Eastern European Emigré League?"

"Yes, for some time now I am member of E.E.E.L. Westchester. We sent letter announcing this new initiative. You did receive this letter?"

"No," she said simply.

He shrugged. "Is unbelievable, the mails here. Can I sit?"

"Yes, please." She cleared some newspapers off the couch and motioned him over.

"I don't do very much with E.E.E.L.," Blanka confided. "I just give them a few dollars now and then when I can."

"A little every year," Barzeny said. "I know. I see records."

"You're Russian?" she asked curiously.

"Yes, I came here in '76." He sat back and looked around the small apartment. "As you know," he continued, "up to now most of efforts of our small organization is to get United States government to put pressure on Eastern Bloc nations to accept Helsinki accords. But now there is much change with this glasnost. So much is happening and E.E.E.L. needs to know what issues members want us to follow. Quota system, easing currency exchange . . . things like this. So, is my job to get you to meet with your Hungarian friends, discuss the situation, and give us your recommendations." He smiled at her. "You have perhaps glass of tea I could have?"

"Certainly," she said. "I could use one too. Just take a second." She got up, went over to a little Pullman kitchen, and turned on the burner under the kettle. In three minutes she came back with two steaming glasses of tea.

"But why me?" she asked, sitting down on the other side of the couch from him. "Why not the people in the organization who are more active and important?"

"We find," Barzeny said, sipping the tea, "that more important means only they donate more money. Money is good, but we need people to donate time." He smiled. "You mind if I ask what it is you do? This information was not on the file card."

"I am a house cleaner. These days, a very busy house cleaner."

"Interesting. Eastern half of Yonkers is my responsibility and I have met many good people. Firemen, nurses, bus drivers. Now house cleaner. I meet famous too. Yesterday I spoke to very famous pianist from Rye." He took another sip from his glass and waited.

"Only famous pianist from Rye I know is Harmon Parrish." Blanka caught her breath. "I should say knew."

"Man that was murdered," Barzeny said in surprise. "You knew him?"

Blanka smiled proudly. "I worked for him. Every Wednesday morning. The poor man never lifted a finger to clean the place, not so much as a simple sweep, so I had a lot to do there. And I suppose I could tell you a few things about him, too.''

Knight takes queen, Barzeny thought. ''I can't believe you worked for him,'' he said, leaning forward. ''This is very big deal. I followed this case closely. I heard on TV, for example, the door wasn't forced. That means he was murdered by someone he knew. Imagine that.'' He lowered his voice. ''Maybe you meet him?''

Mrs. Sologyar fluffed herself out on the coach. ''It's true about the door, although I didn't hear them mention it on the television. But I don't know about meeting anyone who might have killed him. Morning times, when I worked, he was always alone.''

''This man had to have enemies.'' Barzeny tried to sound casual. ''No one is murdered by friends. So you really worked for him?''

She nodded. ''I was the one that found him lying there.'' She shook her head to try to get rid of the thought. ''Oh, there were some occasional excited phone conversations, I'll tell you that. Mr. Parrish, he was kind of the emotional sort. I couldn't help hearing them, I was right there, wasn't I, not like I was prying. Of course, if he was practicing he'd let the phone service get the calls until he was finished.''

''Phone service?'' Barzeny repeated.

''Yes, he hated to be interrupted in the middle of playing.'' She closed her eyes, then after a long moment, opened them again. ''Had a lot of quirks like that. Hated things to be moved from their special places. Cushion on the piano bench had to be centered, the crystal ashtray always to the right, the inlaid box of cigarettes to the left. That's how I knew there was something funny the minute I walked in the door. I saw that the marble box was on the right, which was totally wrong.''

''No doubt you told police what these arguments were about?''

She shook her head. ''I didn't tell the police anything because I didn't know anything. I didn't know who he was talking to or why so I kept quiet.''

"But you knew why," Barzeny prodded. "You told me you heard from phone."

She backtracked. "Well, not clearly enough to point any fingers."

Barzeny sat back. "Well, between you and me," he said, "I think drugs. People always murdered for drugs."

She smiled secretively, then couldn't hold herself in. "Not drugs, money. It was mostly about money."

"For lessons?" Barzeny asked.

"That too."

Barzeny looked quizzical.

Blanka lowered her voice. "Don't tell anyone I said this," she whispered and paused.

Barzeny shrugged. "Of course not, I am here for Eastern European Emigré League."

"Well, then, it was also for something he had. I don't know what it was, but one time I heard him say the money was two weeks late, and if he didn't get it soon he'd have to show what he had. Something like that."

Barzeny smiled. Knight to F3, checkmate! "Blackmail," he said softly.

Blanka squirmed. "Maybe. I don't know. He was always decent to me. Paid me prompt. Police asked me one or two things, but I didn't think I'd do him dirt after he was dead."

"Oh, I understand, Mrs. Sologyar, I understand." He finished the rest of the tea in his glass. "Unless you had names you could help them with."

She searched into Barzeny's wrinkled eyes. Slowly she shook her head. "I wish I did. I truly wish I did."

Barzeny looked at his watch and stood up. "Oh, is very late. We seem to have gotten off track but now I must go," he said quickly. "I have three more people to visit. All Romanians, can you believe it. Please think about what I am asking, meeting with your friends to give us your interests now that things have changed. I will call again soon." He turned toward the door. "And thank you for tea." In the time it took Blanka to bend over and pick up the used glasses, he was gone.

Thirty-one

THERE WAS ONLY ONE TABLE GOING AT McArdle's and it was a slow game at that. Leo and Barzeny were huddled in the corner by the soda machine. In front of the older man was an empty container which had, ten minutes earlier, been filled with Griben's best chicken-and-rice soup. Leo was listening carefully.

"Blackmail killed him, not drugs," Barzeny said. "He was putting, how you say it, nails to someone day before he was killed. Blanka Sologyar heard his end of conversation."

"The screws," Leo corrected. "You amaze me, Jakob. How the hell did you get to her?"

He waved his hand as if the question were a minor thing. "I find out her name from Ingrahm. Then I make guess that she has heard of little group of which I am familiar and where I have a friend. Is easy to see their records and right away we have something in common."

"What else did you get from Ingrahm?" Leo asked hopefully.

"Much." Barzeny nodded. "Our little game turned out better than expected. I let him get away with stalemate and afterwards, we chat. I talked about me in Russia as policeman, and then he takes over." Barzeny winked. "An interesting man, but maybe he is a little indiscreet about his cases. I got Sologyar's name, then Parrish's wound, the fact that he was cocaine user, also that his fingernails were clean of evidence, which I find very interesting." He smiled. "Ingrahm thinks the murder was done by very tall man, and by man who is ambidextrous.'' He drew the word out and sat back. ''I can see how tall you are Leo, but tell me, what is this ambidextrous?''

Leo frowned. "Son of a bitch—you're kidding?''

Barzeny shook his head slowly.

"I am ambidextrous. It means you can use both hands equally well.''

Barzeny continued. ''He got that all from depth and shape of wound. Now you see what police have against you. Plus cuff link.''

"Jesus Christ, I told Rucker that Parrish had stolen them. I can't help it if they only found one.''

"Another piece of their case. Enough pieces and noose draws closer.''

"They don't hang people in New York State, Jakob. Maybe in Russia, but not here.''

"In Russia it's firing squad . . . Officially. Unofficially it can be many things.'' He smiled. "You were being black-mailed by Parrish, maybe, Leo?''

"No,'' Leo said firmly, ''but I think I know who was. A young woman employed by the Eberhards.''

"Is she over six feet tall and ambidextrous?''

"No, but I'll bet she has a friend who is,'' Leo said. ''Parrish was attempting to blackmail the illegal aliens in all the houses where he taught. Either that or sell them drugs. What if one of the maids wouldn't go for either of his deals? She's been working here for over a year, on her way to a green card, and along comes this guy who wants to put her back on the boat if she won't cough up a big chunk of her weekly salary. She gets one of her boyfriends to join her, and the two of them go to see Parrish. Maybe to threaten him to lay off. He opens the door to her because he knows her, and then they argue. One thing leads to another and the boyfriend kills him. So far so good, but things get better. They get lucky and the police right away arrest the wrong person for the murder. They're on easy street, but soon the investigation starts to get closer to the truth as the accused, Leo Perkins, begins asking questions the police overlooked. He finds one maid Parrish attempted to blackmail and is directed towards others. The young woman gets nervous and decides it's time to take a powder, go back home to Ireland until things blow over." Leo sat back. "Theresa Mullins, the Eberhards' maid, unexpectedly left two days ago for the village of Macroom in County Cork." Leo smiled. "Or maybe she just told them she was going there and took off for San Francisco or somewhere else with her boyfriend. This is the same Theresa Mullins who told me she knew Parrish was not so innocent. Now why do you suppose she said that? Because he was blackmailing her. Don't you think it fits?"

Barzeny sat still for a moment and concentrated on a little spot of ink on the tabletop between them. His right hand was in his jacket pocket, playing with the pistachio nuts that were always there. The noise sounded like a muted maraca.

"Is very nice for your defense," Barzeny said. "If they don't find girl it throws what you call shadow of doubt into jury room. In America," he grinned, "shadow of doubt is more important than bright lit-up fact." He pulled his hand out and put one of the nuts between his teeth. He bit down on it until it cracked. "Yes, good for defense, but not logical. Think, Leo, again, why a garrote?"

"Maybe he was familiar with them."

The Russian shook his head. "I think no. That part is important. I think we are missing something. We must see garrote, that and room where he was murdered. Can you get lawyer to arrange it?"

"I'll ask."

"And clean fingernails, Leo. This is not good. No struggle. Someone puts wire around your neck and you don't claw at him?"

"Maybe she held his hands?"

There was a silence in the small space over the table. Finally Barzeny spoke. "I suppose we should follow up your theory. Mrs. Sologyar mentioned to me that Parrish had answering service. Could you get a record of his calls day before he was murdered?"

Leo thought for a moment, then stood up and went over to the pay phone on the wall. Barzeny watched his back as he placed first one call, then another. In two minutes he was back.

"That was easy. I got Parrish's number from information, and when I called the service was still in place answering his phone. His bill was paid until the end of the month, I guess. Anyway, I got the service's address. It's somewhere over in Eastchester."

Barzeny stood up. "So we go. This is like old times."

"For you," Leo said, "but not for me."

Thirty-two

BY THE TIME THEY ARRIVED AT THE AD-vanced Answering Service office it was almost seven o'clock. They rang the doorbell of the run-down single-story building and waited. Next to the front door was a small plastic plaque that advertised to the world what this funny little building was up to . . . answering phone calls by courteous operators. If the man who answered the door was one of their courteous operators, it was no wonder answering machines were so popular.

"Yeah, what do you guys want?" he asked, standing there in a Mets T-shirt with a soda in his hand. "You come to see the boss, come back tomorrow."

"I'll do that," Leo said. "But I wouldn't mind talking to you for a minute if you're not busy." He reached into his wallet and held up a twenty dollar bill. "Maybe it'll stretch as long as five minutes. How about it?"

The short man behind the door looked first at the bill, then at Leo, then at the older man by his side, and made a decision. He turned around and motioned them in. "Sure, buddy, come in and have a seat. If you don't mind being interrupted by my answering phone calls, we can have a nice chat. There are only two of us here anyway, and George is as much fun as a week-old corpse . . . reading all the time." He walked over to one of the many cubicles and sat down at his chair. "Pull over some seats, there's enough room."

The three of them huddled in the small space and Leo leaned closer. "Just a few questions," he began and laid the twenty dollars on the desk. The other man just let it sit.

"How do you guys keep records of incoming calls?"

The man with the soda pointed to a spiral notebook. "In there."

"Mind if I look?"

"Depends," the operator said. "These records are supposed to be confidential." He looked down at the twenty dollars, then back up at Leo. "Supposed to be."

Leo reached into his wallet and fished up another twenty dollar bill. He placed it gently on top of the first one.

"I'm interested in this number: 666-4981. I'd just like to know what calls the number got last week."

The operator looked over at his counterpart three cubicles away who had his nose buried in a motorcycle magazine. "Hold on." He got up and walked over to the office where he checked a master list. "That's desk three," he said when he returned and moved into the cubicle next to the one they were sitting in. "At night we move around, but during the day each one of these phones has an operator." He reached into the top drawer and removed a spiral-bound notebook. "Here we go," he said and dumped the book on his desk. "Keep in mind that a lot of calls come in and when people hear they got the service, they just hang up. They don't say who called or what number or nothing."

"I understand," Leo said and brought the book closer. Barzeny leaned forward and the two of them flipped through the pages. After a minute Barzeny looked up.

"Other numbers in here too?"

"That's right. Each desk takes about fifteen to twenty lines. All the incoming calls are logged with the time and the person who called in a separate section of the book for that particular number. That makes it easier for the operator to give back messages when one of the clients calls. Find the section with your number, then what follows is the day-to-day record.''

''Here it is,'' Leo said and started flipping through the pages quickly. After a few moments he stopped. ''There's no entry here for Tuesday, November fifteenth. Isn't that peculiar?''

''Depends. Some of our clients get only a couple of phone calls a week. Beats me why they take the service at all.''

''But it looks like Parrish got several calls a day. And not one for that day, the day before he died?''

''Or for day later,'' Barzeny said, still looking at the book.

''Maybe he was in both days and picked up himself,'' the operator offered.

''Not likely,'' Leo said. ''He was a piano teacher and spent his afternoons out.''

The operator's eyes got wider, and he put his soda down on the desk top. ''Hey, wait a minute. Are you looking at that guy Harmon Parrish's number, the guy that was killed?'' He pushed his chair back. ''You guys the cops again?''

''They've already been here on this?'' Leo asked.

''Yeah, two days ago cop comes in, wanted to take the book, but my boss wouldn't let him. Told him to copy what he needed because it was easier than us copying fifteen other people's messages. Told him if he wanted the book he needed a subpoena.''

''I think,'' Barzeny said slowly, ''someone beat us. Look, there are rippings inside wire spiral.'' He pointed them out to Leo. ''We are too late. Maybe police.''

''No,'' the employee said. ''I was watching the cop. He didn't rip anything out.''

''Damn,'' Leo said and made a fist. ''The Mullins girl before she took off. We should have acted quicker.''

''Hey, this is getting over my head,'' the operator said and in one motion picked up the book and closed it. ''Maybe you guys ought to talk to my boss about this also.''

Leo looked on the table but the two twenties were gone.

"Come on, Jakob, the murderer got what he wanted."

Barzeny sighed and stood up. "Well, as you say here, at least we are on right track."

"Yeah, but the train's already left the station," Leo said.

Thirty-three

THE NEXT MORNING LEO TOOK AN EARLY lunch break and went down to the county courthouse, part 2, the Honorable Frank Fraley presiding. He slipped quietly into the back of the courtroom and waited patiently for a break in the proceedings. The judge, an imposing black man in even more imposing black robes, was lecturing a young attorney presenting a case before him.

"Mr. Flagstaff," the judge said with some exasperation. "This is the second time today you have come before me with a case that stretches the limits to which our system of justice can distort itself in its toleration of spurious defenses. Now I can appreciate an insanity plea for murder, but I'm afraid there is just no place for it in a larceny case."

"Your honor, he stole the portable five-inch color television set because he was going crazy not being able to watch the Knicks games."

"It won't work, Mr. Flagstaff, and I've been a fan ever since Frazier and Bradley revolutionized the outside game. He also stole a VCR, a Nikon, three watches," the judge flipped some pages, "and a microwave oven. I suppose not being able to have a warm hot dog while he watched the games also contributed to his insanity." A twitter went around the courtroom. "I think you should reconsider your case," the judge continued, "and make some arrangement with the assistant D.A. And in the future, Mr. Flagstaff, let's have a little less creativity and a little more concern for the backlogged calendar of this court." He waited while the lawyer looked down at his client at the table next to him, a young black man wearing a sweatshirt that read SHAKE IT TILL YOU BREAK IT. He looked back up at the judge. "I'm requesting an adjournment," he said resignedly, "for an hour."

The judge looked at his watch and said, "Granted. Thank you. Now we can all have some lunch and hope you come back to your senses on a full stomach." He stood up and turned toward his chambers. The few people in the courtroom started talking to each other as they got up to leave. Leo waited until Flagstaff finished a little discussion with his client, then watched as he walked over to the assistant district attorney's table. They both marked something down in their papers and Flagstaff started up the aisle.

"Sam," Leo said as he approached. "Got a few minutes?"

The young lawyer looked smug. "Hi, Leo. What'd you think?"

"Judge seems to think you're wasting everybody's time."

"All part of the strategy, Leo." He put his arm around him. "All part of the strategy. Get 'em so pissed at you they'll settle for a lesser charge just to get the hell on with it. We just copped a one-to-three instead of what they offered this morning. That insanity thing was just to get them riled." They started walking. "What's up?"

"You got to get us into Parrish's apartment and also get us a look at the murder weapon."

"Us?" Flagstaff said. "I got two more cases this afternoon over here and a bunch over in part one. I can't do it today."

"I don't need you," Leo said. "I have a friend helping me."

The lawyer turned down the corridor to the left.

"Let's go to the cafeteria," he said. "The food's terrible but there's phones and enough noise to have a decent conversation and not worry who's at the next table. What's your friend's name?''

"Barzeny. He used to be a cop . . . in Russia.''

"Marvelous,'' Flagstaff said sarcastically. ''You guys find out anything I should know?''

"Well, I got a theory . . .''

"Good,'' Flagstaff said. "I like theories.'' He smiled. ''Judges hate them.''

Thirty-four

FLAGSTAFF MANAGED TO GET THE APART-
ment unsealed for that afternoon at four. Peterson, unlike Orantes, turned out to be a decent guy and let Leo go early. He drove to McArdle's and picked up Barzeny, and the two of them headed over to Parrish's apartment in one of the nicer sections of Rye. There was a policeman at the door, obviously happy to have pulled an inside detail on a wet and cold November afternoon. But his good spirits did not extend to trusting the enemy, and from the moment the three of them cleared past the yellow crime-scene tape and into the apartment, his eyes never left them. The police were taking no chances on things turning up missing or even new evidence mysteriously appearing. It was Leo's legal right to have a look at the apartment to help in his defense, and that's just what he was getting, and not an inch more. "Look around, but don't mess with the place,'' the cop growled. "If you move something, move it the hell back.''

The first thing that caught Leo's eye was the unexpected opulence of the place. Parrish's rooms were in a neo-Tudor building with a lot of exposed wood beams in the middle of walls and ceilings; and set amongst this dark framework was a decor as modern and expensive as any found in the pages of *Architectural Digest*. There was a white shag rug in the living room, a thick glass coffee table that could have doubled as an ice sculpture, and a marble dining room table Orantes would have swooned over. The only thing that showed a certain vintage was the Steinway in the corner, which looked old but well taken care of. Even the accessories had an expensive look; the marble inlaid box on the right side of the piano with a crystal ashtray in the shape of a teardrop next to it, a sterling silver bowl for fruit on a side table. A lot of money had been spent on the furnishings, more than one would expect a piano teacher had access to. Leo wondered if this thought had struck anyone in the D.A.'s office in their headlong rush to indictment. Barzeny pointed to the corridor leading to the bedroom where the chalk outline of the body could still be seen. "He died there," he said and walked over to the doorway. "Strange . . ." he said and popped a pistachio nut into his mouth. ". . . that he was attacked with garrote in narrow hallway."

"I don't follow you," Leo said.

Barzeny answered, "If I want to kill someone by lifting him off ground by neck for half minute or more, I choose place where he could not use legs, somewhere out in open."

"Stupid murderer," Leo said.

Barzeny's lined face smiled under his taxi cap. "No, Leo, successful murderer." He spit the two empty shells into his hand.

Leo nodded at the thought, then looked down at the black stain on the floor. "Lots of blood. If he'd been moved there'd be a trail of it."

"Yes," Barzeny said. "Perhaps. Still, is peculiar. And how was he dressed?"

"The newspapers had him dressed in his pajamas," Leo said. "He was probably in bed when he got up to answer the door."

"And didn't put on dressing gown?" Barzeny frowned.

"Let us take look," he said and continued down the hall. The policeman followed them.

The bedroom was as lavish as the living room although more eclectic. There was a carved mahogany bedstead with a matching night table, a chaise longue in black leather, some expensive Middle Eastern rugs as wall hangings, and a modern brass lamp fixture that curved out from the far wall. A duplicate brass fixture hung down over the bed for reading. The only item that looked out of place was a broom leaning against one of the walls. The room was tidy except for the bed, which had rumpled sheets, as though someone had just gotten out of it. Both men stepped over to its side. Barzeny looked down, touched the sheet, then grabbed a corner and brought it up to his nose. After a moment he whispered to Leo, "Mrs. Sologyar told to me she comes once a week, on Wednesday mornings . . ."

"So?" Leo said.

"So, if she found body when she came Wednesday," he said, lowering his voice, "then sheets should have been ready for wash. They smell like that to you?"

Leo frowned and sniffed the sheet. Then he rubbed it between two fingers and shook his head. "Not really."

"Not to me either. Rumpled, yes, but clean. There is difference. And where is blanket?" He turned to the police officer who was watching them from the end of the room.

"Were sheets changed?" he asked.

The cop shook his head. "No. Nothing was changed or removed."

Leo pulled the bottom sheet away and looked at the bare mattress. "And no mattress cover?"

"Hey, what are you doing?" the cop yelled. "You guys can't touch anything."

"Don't worry, we'll put it back," Leo said.

Barzeny tucked the sheet back in and stepped back. He looked at the bed, then at the floor around it, then at the ceiling above it. He took a step back toward the bed and squinted up. The ceiling had some peeling paint, and over the bed, screwed into one of the wooden beams, there hung the light fixture from a chain. But there were no scars or stains. Without saying anything he slowly dropped to his knees, then carefully flipped over to his back, and like an auto mechanic, slid himself under the chassis of the bed.

"What are you looking for?" Leo asked.

"Just looking," came the reply. Leo watched as Barzeny's legs sidled up and down the length of the floor under the bed.

"We looked under there," the cop said with a snort. "There's nothing." Still the older man's body slithered along the floor.

"I am too old for this," Barzeny grunted and pulled himself completely under. Leo looked at the cop who was shaking his head. "You guys are crazy," is all he said.

"*Govno!*" Barzeny shouted and rattled the bed. "I caught my sleeve. Leo, come and help pull spring away."

Leo joined his friend under the mattress.

"Where?" he asked.

Barzeny held a finger up to his lips and pointed to the rail along the far wall. With his other hand he was deliberately rattling the springs of the bed. Leo followed his finger and saw that he was pointing to a little rectangle of white fabric draped over the top of the wooden rail. He pushed in closer and saw, in the dimmer light under the bed, that it was one of the mattress tags that said UNDER PENALTY OF LAW THIS TAG CANNOT BE REMOVED . . . and gave its content and origin. Leo looked over at Barzeny with questioning eyes. "Just a minute, I'll see if I can release you," he said. The older man brought his mouth closer to Leo's ear and whispered.

"Mattress tags belong on mattresses, not on beds." Slowly he reached out and pulled a corner of it up. The tag peeled away easily from the spot of rubber cement holding it down. Barzeny removed it from the top of the rail but left it hanging by a small strip. He rattled the bed once more, then the two men slid in another few inches to see what the tag had been covering. The rail was an inch wide and made of solid mahogany, but in the middle a narrow groove about two-and-a-half inches long had been cut with some kind of rotary saw. It was very clean, with sharp edges, and almost invisible. Inside the dark slit something metallic glinted up at them.

"You got a problem?" the policeman called.

"No, I think I got it," Leo replied and rattled the bed. Barzeny reached into his pocket and pulled out a small penknife. With the skill of a surgeon performing microsurgery, he inserted the thin blade into the slit, applied sideways pressure, and carefully lifted the penknife back up. Both men saw the top of a thin flat key appear before the blade of Barzeny's knife lost its grip and the key dropped back down into its hiding place.

The policeman dropped to his knees. "I got a wire cutter in the car if you need it," he said. "Let me see."

Leo backed out quickly, bumping into the uniformed man. "No, it's okay." He turned around and leaned against the bed, cutting off Barzeny from view. "Sure is dusty down there."

"You guys . . ." the cop muttered and went over to sit on one of the chairs. Barzeny coughed, spent another fifteen seconds rooting around, then slowly emerged from under the bed.

"Nothing," he said out loud. "Let's look at the rest of the place." They brushed past the policeman and moved on down the corridor and into the kitchen.

"You coming?" Leo said to the cop. "I wouldn't want you to accuse us of stealing some pretzels."

"Buzz off," the cop said, following them.

They didn't find anything of interest in the kitchen or in the bathroom, and in another half hour they decided to leave. The older man looked deep in thought as they emerged from the elevator and out into the cold.

"You get it?" Leo asked softly.

The old Russian nodded and placed the key in Leo's hand. Both of them looked down at it and the words SARGENT AND GREENLEAF INC. written across its top.

"Bank safety deposit box," Leo said.

Barzeny shrugged. "In Russia safes are rare. No one has anything to keep locked up. Does it have address?"

"They never do, that's the problem."

"So we do investigation. Can't be so many banks in neighborhood."

Leo shook his head. "I'm afraid to find out." He reached

into his pocket and withdrew his own key ring. He held out one key for Barzeny to see, a key shaped like Parrish's but bearing the legend MOSLER. "Keys like this all look alike. Could be a hundred places he rented the box. Besides, it's illegal entering a box not your own."

"It is also illegal withholding evidence, no?" Barzeny smiled and cracked a nut between his back teeth. "But we say nothing about it yet."

Leo pocketed Parrish's key.

"What about that other stuff?" Leo asked. "The clean sheets and no blanket?"

"I am not sure," the Russian said. "But I think maybe he was not killed in hallway." He started walking toward Leo's car. "When can we see garrote? Good policeman always must see murder weapon."

"Flagstaff is going to let me know."

"Maybe tomorrow morning we try to find Mr. Parrish's safe box. I meet you at the club at ten?" He raised his eyes questioningly.

"Sure, I think I can stretch my boss for a couple of hours."

"Good. See you then," Barzeny said quietly and took a step away. He looked like a lonely old man shuffling off to a lonely cold night.

Leo asked, "Jakob, why are you doing all this?"

The other man turned, looked at Leo, and said simply, "Just protecting my stamp collection." Then he turned and walked away into the rainy evening.

Thirty-five

WITHOUT THE GRUMBLING AND KIBITZ-
ing of the players, McArdle's was silent and lifeless the next
morning. Leo found Barzeny by the pay telephone reading
an old telephone directory. He pulled over a chair and sat
down next to him.

Barzeny began in a tired voice. "In your capitalist state
you have more banks than schools."

"By my count," Leo added, "over sixty branches in a
five-mile radius of Harmon's apartment. I was up last night
looking also." He pulled from his pocket a piece of paper
with several listings and smoothed it out on his knees. "It's
hopeless," he continued. "We can't try each one. I've narrowed it down to the ten nearest him. Maybe we'll get lucky."

"I don't believe in luck," the older man said. "Is another
capitalist invention. I never won a chess game because of
it."

"Tell that to the thousands of lottery winners," Leo said
with a smile. He took out Parrish's key and held it out. "I
can't figure any other way. "Sargent and Greenleaf Inc," he
read off. "It could be any one of them."

"So," Barzeny said with a sigh. "We give it a try. Hard
work makes for what you call luck. You have a plan of attack?"

"A scenario," Leo said. "I'll tell you in the car. But first
you have to practice this signature." He pulled out an invitation to a recent concert at the County Center with the hand-
written inscription *Hope you can make it, Harmon Parrish*

113

and put it on the table in front of him. "It doesn't have to be perfect, just close enough to pass a casual inspection."

"So, now you making me into forger, Leo. That is not nice." Barzeny leaned over the scrap of paper and studied the writing.

"What about taking chances, Jakob? Is that another capitalist invention?"

The older man laughed and picked up a pen Leo held ready. "No," he said, "is universal." He bent low over the paper and practiced Parrish's small handwriting. Twenty minutes later the two men got up and left the club.

The First National Bank of Rye was the closest branch to Parrish's apartment. It was located three blocks away, on Purchase Street, and was, as far as suburban banks go, an imposing edifice. Freshly painted white columns straddled a Federal-style entrance and led into a large banking floor. Along with five tellers, there were two middle-aged women officers working the platform behind a low rail. At ten-thirty in the morning no one was waiting, and Leo and Jakob pushed through the little gate. Immediately one of the women looked up and motioned them over. Barzeny held out the key and said softly, "Safety deposit, please." The woman smiled, one of those two hundred throw-away smiles she had inventoried for the day, and stood up. She took a few steps over to the wall where there was a small box of cards on file.

"Name, please?" she said and held out her hand for the key.

Barzeny dropped it into her palm and said, "Parrish," then held his breath. Leo was standing right behind him.

"Paritch?" she asked after a moment. "I don't see any listing for that name."

Barzeny spelled it out for her: "P-A-R-R-I-S-H." Still she looked but ran through the box without stopping.

"No," she concluded. "Not here." Then she got an inspiration and looked down at the key. "This isn't even our key. I think you have the wrong bank, sir." She gave the key back out to Barzeny.

"I told you, Dad, this didn't look like the right one. It's

the one over on Tuckahoe Road. Come on.'' Leo took Barzeny's sleeve and directed him out of the little platform area where the officers sat. "Sorry for the trouble," he said over his shoulder to the woman who had been helping them. "At his age . . ." He pointed to his head. "You know what I mean." The two of them exited the bank and headed for Leo's car.

"One down," Jakob said, "Fifty-nine to go."

Five banks later the game was wearing thin. At four establishments there was a replay of what happened at the first bank, and at their last stop, the officer had taken only a glance at the key before calling a halt to the proceedings. When they stepped into the Westchester Savings and Loan Branch at Highland Avenue it was already eleven-thirty, and both Leo and Barzeny were tired and frustrated.

"Safety deposit box," Barzeny said once again to the bank clerk, this time a young man dressed for success in a pinstripe suit.

"Name, please?" he asked perfunctorily and turned to the side of his desk where the records were kept.

"Parrish," the older man said and placed the key on the man's desk. Mr. Pinstripe looked at it, then went to the records.

"You know your box number, Mr. Parrish?"

Barzeny shook his head. "I forget these things," he said simply. "Not often I come."

The clerk smirked. "Once a week by this record," he said. "I'm new here or I'm sure I'd recognize you." He handed Jakob the little form.

Barzeny signed, then straightened up while the clerk looked at the signature. Leo took a step closer.

"Could you wait a minute?" the clerk said after a long moment. His voice had a harder edge to it. He got up and walked slowly over through a door marked ROBERT ELLIS, v.p. Barzeny looked toward Leo who now had a frown on his face.

"I don't like this," Leo whispered. He bent over and retrieved the key still on the man's desk and slipped it into his pocket. Then he quickly undid his own key on its separate one-inch ring and put it in its place.

A phone rang somewhere off to the right, and Leo saw a bank guard walk over and pick it up. The guard nodded twice, glanced over at them, and ambled off in the direction of the front door. Then two men exited from the rear office. Mr. Pinstripe still held the signature card. Mr. Ellis looked determined.

"Mr. Parrish," Ellis began. "I'd like a word with you."

Barzeny smiled and said, "Paris. Name is Paris, P-A-R-I-S. Short for Parisnikov. You have problem?"

"Yes, there's a problem. You're claiming to be Harmon Parrish, a man who died several days ago. I'd say that's fraud. I don't know what the police will say when they get here."

"One moment," Barzeny said softly. "It is you who have made mistake. I do not know this Mr. Parrish. My name is Harry Paris. You can see from card I signed. See here," he pointed to the card, "one R, no H. My son told me this is not bank I start safety box in two years ago, but I disagreed. Must be I was mistaken."

"He did sign Paris, not Parrish," Mr. Ellis said, now looking closer.

"He's lying, the key is ours," Pinstripe said. "It's right here." He picked up Leo's key with the steel ring.

"I would be careful who I was accusing of lying," Leo said, taking a step closer. "Especially senior citizens making an honest mistake." Mr. Ellis glanced quickly at the younger bank clerk. "Is that your key?" Leo continued.

Ellis took a step closer to look at the key and scowled. "Crowley, that's a Mosler, it's not ours. Goddammnit, you've made a mistake. Your second this week."

"But it wasn't that key he gave me, it was a Sargent and Greenleaf, I'm sure. You'll find it if you search him."

"This is not Russia, Mr. Crowley," the vice-president said sternly.

"I'd thank you to apologize to my father," Leo chimed in, "after you give him back the key."

"Crowley, apologize," Ellis commanded and turned on his heel. "Then I want to see you."

"I'm sorry," Pinstripe said. After a long moment he held the key out. "But it was a Sargent and Greenleaf key."

Leo took the Mosler key and said evenly, "Tell your guard to let us by." The scowling clerk gave the guard a sign and then turned toward his appointment with Ellis in the corporate woodshed. Leo and Jakob hurried out.

"What made you make it Paris and not Parrish?" Leo asked when they were back in the car.

"Caution," Barzeny said. "Or I think what your young people call here vibrations. In Russia, tuning in to vibrations is way of life."

"I've got to get back to work," Leo said. "I'll take the key with me and find someplace at Rivetz to hide it."

"Maybe it's not such good idea to keep it?"

Leo shrugged. "I hate to throw things away. You never know when they might come in handy."

Thirty-six

FLAGSTAFF WAS WAITING FOR THEM OUTside Rucker's office early the next morning. The weather had cleared and a cold November morning had the heat on fullblast in the colorless, low-ceilinged rooms of the ten-yearold police station. Rucker showed the three of them inside and pointed to a side table.

"You wanted to see the weapon, there it is," he said abruptly. "It's already been dusted so you can handle it." He went back to his desk and fumbled with some papers in the way people do when they want to look busy. But his eyes under the dark eyebrows darted back and forth from his desk to the three men as they walked over to the table. The garrote inside the plastic evidence bag was a nasty piece of work. Like shivs cut from prison bedsprings, or zip guns from car aerials, or metal knuckles from hammered battery lead, it spoke of both the cruelty and ingenuity of man. It was a simple length of piano wire attached to cut-off broomstick handles. Crude, banal, yet very effective. The dried blood-stain on the middle of the wire said it all. Flagstaff took one look and turned away. But Barzeny picked up the contraption and brought it close to his face. He squinted at the stainless eyehooks through which the wire was attached to the wood, measured the thickness of the wire through his fingers, looked at the rough-cut ends of the handles, and felt the weight. When he was finished he handed the weapon to Leo, who also looked at it carefully and replaced it in the bag.

"Satisfied?" Rucker asked, his eyes apparently focused on a piece of paper on his desk. He looked up slowly. "Perhaps you'd also like to see the pajamas he was wearing," he said sarcastically. "Calvin Klein."

"Where was blanket?" Barzeny asked quietly. "A cold night in November and no blanket on his bed?"

Rucker leaned back. "Who's he?"

"An investigator on my staff," Flagstaff said, covering for the scruffy-looking little man. "He was with my client at Parrish's apartment. His name is Jakob Barzeny."

"The blanket," Barzeny persisted. "There was none?"

"Look at the evidence report or the pictures," Rucker said. "You think I can remember every detail? I'm sure Mr. Flagstaff here already asked for a set of prints. But what's the difference, blanket, no blanket? We have your client Perkins cold."

"I think not," Flagstaff said. "One of the reasons we came in was to see the weapon. The other was to give you a message for the D.A." He looked carefully at the police officer. "Juries don't like loose ends, Lieutenant Rucker. Doubts," he touched his forehead dramatically, "the kind district attorneys hate to see on jurors' minds, spring from unresolved loose ends." He leaned forward. "We are facing a case here with more loose ends than an oriental rug. I'm sure you're not aware of all of them, but here's one I'm going to give you on a platter. Why has one of the people Harmon Parrish was either extorting or supplying drugs to mysteriously disappeared? A loose end," Flagstaff said softly, "as big as a stallion's pecker."

Rucker narrowed his eyes. It was a moment before he said anything. "Who was that?"

"Theresa Mullins, the Eberhards' maid. Either you find her or your case against my client isn't worth a nickel . . . not even a taxpayer's nickel." He got up and motioned Barzeny and Perkins to follow. "We'll be in touch," he said before leaving.

Outside on the pavement Barzeny broke into a broad grin. "Very good. In chess is always best to attack when opponent is unbalanced."

"Hell, it's just cheaper for them to find her than it is for us. For all I know she could be cutting alfalfa right now in County Cork."

"Hardly," Leo said. "She wasn't the type."

They walked slowly to Flagstaff's car, a gleaming new Audi 5000. The car was ten feet away from the next one in the lot, but the young lawyer opened its door with the care he would give a piece of fine crystal. The three men settled themselves inside and Flagstaff pulled out.

"Leo's being framed," Barzeny said, "and that policeman is too stupid to see it." He leaned back into the soft leather of the new-smelling car and closed his eyes. After a moment he started reciting:

> Half hero and half ignoramus
> What's more, half scoundrel, don't forget
> But on this score the man gives promise
> That he will make a whole one yet.

He opened his eyes. "Pushkin. Things were no different in 1824. Yes, Leo is being framed and by very clever person. Someone like Alekhine in the twenties when he was sacrificing bishops at will." He opened Flagstaff's ashtray and unceremoniously unloaded a pocketful of pistachio shells into its spotless interior. At the noise Flagstaff turned and gave him a nasty look. "We have things to talk about," Barzeny continued.

"I have to get to work," Leo protested.

"Leo, this is very serious, unless you want work to be breaking rocks for rest of your life. They do that here, don't they?"

"In the movies," the lawyer said.

"And I can't think on empty stomach," Barzeny announced, pointing to a foul-looking diner wedged in between two parking lots.

Flagstaff turned the wheel and the car glided to the curb. When he pulled the key out of the ignition he just sat for a moment appreciating the way the new car was shutting its many systems down. In a few minutes the three men were nursing steaming cups of coffee.

"Let us be logical," Barzeny began, motioning to the waitress. The middle-aged, overly made-up woman came to the table and Barzeny pointed. "What is that?"

The waitress peered over to where he was pointing. "Them's sticky buns."

"Sticky buns?" he repeated as though she had just recited his personal mantra. "Sticky buns. I take two." He rubbed his hands together. "Now, here is logic as I see it. This maid has disappeared. Why? Maybe because of something she knew. Maybe she turns up dead somewhere, or maybe she just was given money to go home and forget about awkward situation . . . lot of money." His eyes perked up at the sight of the waitress returning with two sticky buns. He took a bite, then continued. "Now, what could maid who is stuck in large mansion know to make her dangerous enough to kill or bribe?"

"Who murdered Parrish," Flagstaff said flatly.

"Yes, and who does that point to?" Barzeny said.

"Eberhard." This time it was Leo.

"Point of logic number one," the old chess master said and took another bite of the rich honey bun. "Point of logic number two. I think to teach piano is second only to teaching chess in how much effort goes in and how little money comes out. But Parrish's apartment showed us different. Man was *bogach*, he had lots of bucks. But now we know that where this man taught he also stole, blackmailed, sold drugs, or did other illegal things. Is obvious that Parrish taught only where he could make extra money. Now, Leo was told nothing was taken from Eberhards' when he called right after cuff links were missing. This leaves big possibility he was extorting at that house.'' He took a breath.

"Eberhard," Leo supplied.

Barzeny nodded. "Point of logic number three. In looking at evidence you must be detective, chemist, engineer, and physicist. We learn this in Russia before we become policemen. Example, German spy is caught trying to enter Leningrad during '43 siege with false papers. How did Russian colonel inspecting documents know they were false?'' He finished the last bite of the sticky bun. "Because unlike Russian staples, during war German staples are chromium plated, leave no rust marks. The papers the spy carried had been put together in Berlin.'' He sat back. "Spy was shot.''

"What does that have to do with Parrish's murder?'' Flagstaff asked.

"Eyehooks of the garrote made out of stainless steel. In America are stainless-steel hooks found in every house toolbox?'' He smiled at Leo. "I think not, unless you plan to be around water, say in sailboat.''

"Eberhard," Leo breathed again.

"Finally," Barzeny continued, "Dr. Ingrahm told me that murder was committed by someone very tall like you, Leo. So I am curious to know how tall this Eberhard is?''

"Tall enough to adjust the telltales on his sailboat," Leo recalled. "I'd say he was as tall as I am.''

Barzeny concluded. "Logic point number four. Everything goes in one direction. That is good part. The bad part is that police do not seem interested in logic, especially when it points to very important man in community. It is up to us.'' He held up his cup to the waitress and waited for her to come over with more coffee.

"Okay, what about the blanket?'' Leo asked. "And the sheets?''

"What sheets?" Flagstaff asked.

Barzeny grinned. "Obvious Parrish was killed on bed where he bled like a hog. Blood there was carefully removed. Why, I do not know yet."

Barzeny started as Leo's watch announced with an invasive set of blips that it was ten o'clock. "Christ, I've got to run," Flagstaff said, looking at his own watch. "I should be in court now." He threw a five dollar bill on the table and grabbed his coat. "Call me later," he said to Leo.

Barzeny looked down wistfully at the five dollars after the lawyer had left, then finally decided. "I think I take some eggs," he said. "Too early for lunch, no?"

"Still breakfast," Leo agreed. "But I can only stay for five minutes. I've been out so much this week I'll be surprised if I get a paycheck. Besides, to Rivetz from here by bus has got to be over twenty minutes. What did you have in mind?"

"Poached. I love poached eggs."

"No, I mean about Eberhard?"

"Oh." Jakob frowned. "I have idea, but we need help. Telephone records were stolen from answering service. Why? Because whatever was written down was too dangerous. So Eberhard took them, but we need to convince him that there are copies."

"There are?" Leo asked.

"Not exactly," the chess master said. He winked and raised his hand to the waitress again. Leo sighed and sank back into the vinyl upholstery of the booth.

"I keep telling you, Leo," the older man said, "what you need most is patience. It leads to success in many things, not only in game of chess."

"So," Leo said with a forced smile, "I'll wait."

Thirty-seven

BY THE TIME LEO ARRIVED AT RIVETZ'S, PE-
terson was past looking annoyed.

"Of all days you gotta be late," he opened up, "today's
leather sectionals. Our goddamn inventory on leather sectionals is bigger than it is on paper clips. Two hours late,
Leo?"

"Sorry," Leo said. "I was just going over some details
of my defense. It isn't easy."

"I know, buddy, but comes the point when we got a business to run here." He handed Leo a clipboard. "I started in
on aisle J, but I can't do two jobs. Can you stay late?"

Leo nodded. "I guess I have to. And thanks."

"Oh yeah, Orantes was out arranging for that marble table
to be moved into the showroom next week. In case you're
interested, he told me they pulled Jansen over from Patio on
a permanent basis, so maybe you shouldn't be looking for
your old job back."

Leo didn't say anything and started to walk away. He
headed into the part of the warehouse where the sectionals
were kept and started his count against the inventory sheet.
But his mind wasn't on couches. He wanted to find Sollie
and ask him something. And then, sometime later when he
had a breather, he'd walk on over to aisle O and check on the
table, as he had every afternoon since he'd rigged the packing
timber. That fucking Orantes.

He found Sollie later eating lunch alone and reading the
Daily News. Leo said, "Hey, I forgive you."

Sollie raised his head. "What the hell for?"

"For being such an asshole about your precious gun collection when I needed help. But hey, I understand. You couldn't be sure I'd make my court appearance. You've only known me what, fifteen years?"

Sollie looked sheepish and bent back into his newspaper.

"But just to show you there are no hard feelings, I'm going to let you do me a favor. I'm going to let you loan me a gun."

"Very generous of you," Sollie said, not looking up. "What'd you have in mind? Something for deer?"

"No, something for bigger game." He let that sit for a moment. "What I had in mind has to fit inside a glove compartment. You got something like that in your collection?"

"A handgun? Christ, Leo, what do you want a handgun for?" He put the paper down.

"If I told you self-defense, would you believe me?"

Sollie was silent for a moment.

"Maybe." He studied Leo. "You really need it?"

Leo nodded. "You can get away with being a prick once, but not twice."

"Okay," Sollie finally decided. "I got a Smith and Wesson model 29 .44 magnum I used to drop boar with out in California. I'll bring it in tomorrow." He leaned back.

Leo stood up and placed his hand on Sollie's shoulder. "Thanks, Sollie. I was hoping you would come through."

The other man looked up at him and his face flushed. "Leo, I'm sorry, I was wrong about the bail. But I hope you know what you're doing."

He called Barbara and told her he was staying at Rivetz an extra two hours. Then he climbed steel cages all afternoon, squeezing between stacked couches, peering inside packing crates, and checking off what he found on his clipboard. It took him an hour to track down the ottoman to a Black Bayou four-piece sectional that had been placed in with the Black Impala collection. By seven-thirty the store's doors had closed and the salesmen had gone home. The security department's two night men moved out into their assigned areas, one for the vast warehouse and one for the interior of the store. Leo nodded at the one who passed him and raised his clipboard to show what he was up to. Then he went back to the final bins to be checked on his report.

When he was finished he placed the sheets of paper with a paper clip on Peterson's desk, then detoured to aisle O. There it sat, still looking like the flight deck of the USS *Forrestal*, a dining table that weighed more than a car. The packing timber was no longer propped up against one of the legs. Leo figured it was time to stop leaving things up to chance and start thinking more creatively.

The bin over the marble table held a small coffee table, but there was plenty of room in front of it. He had seen something nearby that would fit perfectly. Row 4, second bin from the floor, a bin with two large marble cylinder lamps to match a set of marble end tables. He walked the few feet over and used the movable ladder to get one of them down. The lamp was a solid piece of marble ten inches in diameter and two feet long that weighed, not including the shade, every bit of sixty pounds. After moving the lamps, Leo lifted out a shelf from a nearby wooden bookcase. The last thing he needed was a piece of cardboard, which he found in the back of a nearby bin. The idea was very simple but the execution would have to be precise. He set the shelf in place running from the back of the bin to the front and placed a doubled-over piece of cardboard at the edge farthest into the bin, raising it just enough to create a gradual inclined plane. Then he placed one marble lamp without its shade crosswise on the shelf and wedged it in place with another doubled-over piece of cardboard the size of a book of matches. The second lamp went in back of the first one. There were now one hundred and twenty pounds of marble sitting on an imperceptibly inclined piece of wood being held in check by a flimsy cardboard wedge. The regular vibrations from the metal frame building would be enough to move the cardboard down the wood shelf so that within two or three days the lamps would fall and land on the outer edge of the marble table beneath them. Shattered marble everywhere, Leo figured. Then he gave the metal bin a tiny shake and watched as the two lamps slid down an inch before pinching the cardboard and coming to a rest again. Perfect, he thought, and walked away.

Thirty-eight

BUT WHAT HAD BEEN BOTHERING HIM ALL day throughout the inventory count came back to haunt him on the drive home. Barzeny had put his finger on it. Parrish taught only where there were special opportunities, so why his house? Surely not for one lousy pair of cuff links after three months.

Amanda was busy with her homework when Leo entered the house. Barbara had the dishes cleared away and had a plate ready for him in the microwave. Very neat, very efficient, very confusing. Ever since Parrish's murder Barbara had been changing subtly. He noticed it when she started cutting back on the cigarettes. Then she was watching less television and taking care of the house better. Even the outfits she wore seemed to be chosen more carefully. It was the kind of sea change a person goes through when something happens to make them think better of themselves . . . like when they enter into a new relationship, or in the case of a married woman, when she starts having an affair. So, what was it? The arrest and impending trial of her husband? Would that cause a switch away from TV dinner meat loaf to home-cooked honey-glazed ham? Why? To show the world they still had a family? Or was it something else? Here he was, wriggling on the end of a line like a gut-hooked catfish, and maybe the person on the other end holding the pole was his wife. He made himself a stiff drink, turned the microwave oven on full, and sat down next to Barbara at the kitchen table. Ten minutes, he figured, was all she could take watching the honey glaze melting out of the cracks in the door. Ten minutes to get the truth.

He swallowed a mouthful of the bourbon and told her not to get up until they had finished talking. "I'll take care of the oven."

She pointed at the timer. "You know you've put it on full power for forty minutes. The meat will explode by then." She had a smile on her face but her eyes kind of questioned his.

"A new taste sensation," he said. "Let's talk."

"About what?"

"About Parrish?"

She looked at the microwave, then back at Leo. "What about him?"

"I want to know what the hell he had on you. You told me you weren't screwing him and I believe you. But there must be something else. What does Rucker have that he won't give up on me?"

She shrugged. "What could he have?" Her eyes held him. "You tell me."

"He taught our daughter piano, that's all."

The steady hum of the microwave oven's fan filled the silence that followed. "I've never seen a ham explode, Barbara," Leo stated, "but there's always a first time."

"You're acting like a child."

"Children aren't indicted for murder, Barbara. I'm trying to defend myself, but I can't do it unless I know all the facts. Parrish had a reason for coming here other than Amanda's little lesson, and unless you tell me what that was I'm going to prison." The timer on the oven had dropped to thirty-seven minutes.

"Leo, the microwave was two hundred and fifty dollars." Her voice was a notch louder. "That's two days for you at Rivetz. Not to mention the ham and the two hours it took me to prepare. I think you're being a little melodramatic."

"Maybe I am," he said, watching her. "And maybe I just like my meat well done."

She took a deep breath and peered at the oven. If she had any intentions of switching off its controls, Leo dispelled them by moving his chair closer to the counter. She turned away.

"You won't like it," she said at last.

"I don't expect to," he said, "but I'll like it even less if it's dropped on my head at the trial. Whatever it is, we'll work it out, Barbara. But we can't start unless you're willing to face it. Was it drugs?"

She shook her head. "No, he handled my bets." She said it so softly Leo leaned forward to catch the end of it.

"He what?"

"Handled my bets. He was my bookie." She looked him full in the face now. "I gambled, Leo, I gambled a lot. I took money from you for the house, for clothes and food, and bought the cheapest stuff I could and put the rest on horses. I even hocked some of the jewelry you gave me. I studied the sheets while you were at work, then I made my bets for the week on Tuesdays and sometimes on Fridays with Harmon." She smiled sadly. "I wasn't so bad, actually. I had some very good days, but lately I was losing a lot."

"How much?" Leo said.

"The week before Harmon was murdered I lost five hundred." She looked down at her outstretched fingers resting on the table. "All on some stupid horse called Our Romance that I thought was a sure thing." She shook her head. "I'm sorry, Leo, I knew how you felt about gambling, about the jewelry you gave me. I couldn't let you know. It was kind of a disease after a while, and Harmon didn't make it easier. Every Tuesday he was here and made it so accessible."

"And Fridays?" Leo leaned forward.

She shrugged. "We met at some restaurant over in White Plains. I think it was called the Acapulco Lounge. It was near one of his lessons and we'd have lunch and I'd give him the money and my bets. That was all." She looked into Leo's eyes. "You've got to believe me, that's as far as it went . . . only bets. I didn't think it was important, I mean I didn't think it had anything to do with his murder or your defense. I was debating whether to tell you."

Leo got up and walked to the window. "Jesus Christ, Barbara. Suppose someone saw you at that restaurant with him." He turned on her and the sadness in his eyes wounded her.

"Gambling . . ." He shook his head. He came back to the table. "Damn it, Barbara, if you were so hooked," he continued, "why didn't you go to OTB? Why bet with a roach like Parrish who had half a dozen scams going at one time?"

"Why? Because I didn't want any of our friends to see me enter there. It's right next to the supermarket in the mall. Just down from the wallpaper store, the hairdresser." She stood up and walked over to the microwave oven. He watched as she turned off the timer and opened the door. "It wouldn't have looked right for Amanda's mother to be rubbing elbows with the degenerates at the OTB parlor. Believe me, I know. The ladies at the last PTA meeting were all talking about Christina Freemont's mother who was spotted coming out of the adult book store over on Elm Street. The parents of Amanda's friends would have been shocked. Besides, I didn't want you to find out, especially about the stuff I pawned." She took a deep breath. "But now it's over." She turned around and brought the plate with the ham back over to the kitchen table. "Harmon's dead and I've stopped gambling. And if you really want to know, I feel a lot better. I hated the anxiety of the whole thing, but most of all, I hated the deception. And it never would have stopped if he hadn't been killed. In a way, whoever murdered him did me a favor. I know that's awful to say . . ."

Leo walked over and stood next to her. Slowly he brought his hand up, then put it on her shoulder. He was silent for a moment. "You have incredibly bad timing," he said finally.

She nodded.

"And I'm not sure it takes me off the hook. Rucker might have me murdering Parrish to get you out from under."

"I didn't owe him any money, Leo. I swear. I paid up every cent."

"It still won't look good. And yet . . ." he shrugged and

pulled her closer. "It's better than what they assume they have now. I just don't know what to think."

"How about," she said softly, "you don't think anything? How about you eat?"

Thirty-nine

LEO BEGAN TO PUT BARZENY'S PLAN INTO operation the next morning. Over breakfast . . . with Amanda. Barbara was there, but she held herself in check through the whole discussion, afraid to say one word because she knew that if she began, she'd end up vetoing the whole thing. Using Amanda to flush out her friend's father was bad enough; placing himself in grave danger was going way overboard. When he had told her the idea the night before, she had thought it a long shot. Now, as she listened, she thought it was even worse; it was out-and-out crazy.

"But Daddy," Amanda protested, "Constance didn't invite me over for a study date after school this week."

"That, sweetheart, is where all the effort your mother has put into making you a charming and gracious young lady will pay off." Leo looked at his wife. "You'll arrange things so she does."

"I can't just do that," Amanda said, blushing. "She's not my best friend, you know."

"But you do take classes together and you could easily invite her here, right?"

"I guess so."

"So do that, then at the last moment remember that the painters are coming to do the kitchen that day and look annoyed and suggest that maybe you could go to her house instead. But it's got to be a night when her parents will be home." He smiled at her.

"How come?"

"So you can have dinner with them."

"Daddy!"

"Hey, once you're there, that's the easy part, especially if our kitchen's being painted. If they don't suggest it on their own, maybe you can start looking hungry around six o'clock. Come on, Amanda, when your friends come over we usually ask them to stay."

"That's different," Amanda said. "Constance's family usually has more . . ." she searched for a word, ". . . more serious dinners. You know what I mean? You don't just sit down there to a macaroni casserole, it's more like individual rainbow trout almondine or chicken Kiev, or something like that." She stole a guilty glance at her mother.

Leo's eyes widened. "Where'd you learn about dishes like that?"

Amanda smiled. "I'm twelve years old, you know."

"So, they wouldn't have an extra trout swimming around somewhere in their private stocked pond? Come on, Amanda, you can try."

"What for?" she said. "Why do I have to have dinner with them?"

"Because it's very important that you mention something at the table in all candor and quite naturally or else they might not believe it's true." He sat back. "But ultimately, Amanda honey, because if you don't there's a good chance that, innocent as I am, I might wind up as a guest of Governor Cuomo in one of his prisons." He winked at her. "We wouldn't want that, would we?"

"Well, I'd have one less parent bugging me about homework."

Barbara, over by the refrigerator, let out a tiny chuckle.

"No more skating on frozen ponds upstate," Leo said. "No more late-night Scrabble games, which you always win. No more PG-thirteen movies that your mother wouldn't dream of letting you see . . ."

"Okay, okay," Amanda said. "I'll try it. But there's no guarantee it's going to work."

"There's never a guarantee. You can only do your best."

"So," Amanda said after taking a last swallow of her orange juice. "What is it you want me to say at the Eberhards' dinner table?"

Leo looked at his watch. "The ten minutes it takes to drive you to school should just about do it. By the time I drop you off you'll have it perfectly."

"Good," Amanda said. "But for this I'm raising the stakes."

Leo frowned. "To what?" he asked.

"R-rated movies. I've outgrown all the PG-thirteen."

Forty

THE DINING ROOM HAD A MARBLE FLOOR, which, in Amanda's eyes, said it all. The porcelain urns on the sideboard or the delicate Limoges table settings were pretty, and Amanda guessed they were costly, but the marble floor was truly humbling. It made Amanda think extra hard about all the times her mother had drilled her on table etiquette. Was she supposed to leave the tiny fork on her plate after the salad or put it back where she found it? God, and what about the napkin ring? She'd never even seen one of those before.

"How do you like the soup, Amanda dear?" Mrs. Eberhard asked. "It's not often we get to have some of Mrs. Chiller's turtle soup."

Amanda quickly glanced across the table at Constance,

who was wrinkling up her nose, having just sampled the offending substance.

"It's quite good," Amanda said and struggled with keeping her own face from contorting. "Strong."

"Yes, it is," continued Mrs. Eberhard. "It has to be to set up the venison. Too weak and the meat will come on too abruptly. The turtle soup introduces it nicely, don't you think, Bradford?" She turned to her husband, who was at the head of the table, absorbed in his own thoughts.

"What?"

"I was asking about the soup," Mrs. Eberhard continued. "Don't you think it's a good choice before the venison?"

"I'll let you know when I try the stuff," he said. "You girls having a study date?" He looked at Amanda and he didn't look pleased.

Constance answered, "That's right, Daddy, we're having a history test next week and Amanda thought it would be a good idea if we quizzed each other."

Her father took a spoonful of his soup. "History, huh? Who was it that said, 'Those who forget history are going to have to relive it'? Someone famous, I think maybe Henry Ford." He looked more closely at his daughter's friend. "Lousy business your father's up against. I hope he's got a good lawyer."

Amanda put her soup spoon down. At twelve she knew an opening when she came across it.

"Yes, he does, quite good. His lawyer and he have found a way to prove he's innocent."

"Really?" Mr. Eberhard said casually and tried another spoonful of soup. "How?"

Amanda looked down at the beautifully chased napkin ring, stags running after a dog, or maybe it was the other way around. "Well, I don't know if I'm really supposed to say anything. He was talking to Mom in the living room last night and I guess I overheard."

"Oh, come on Amanda," Constance said. "It's no fair if you brought it up. Cindy Rayburn is always doing that and I hate her for it."

Amanda looked at her friend and giggled. "I'm not even

sure I got what they were talking about. My dad was going on about the police overlooking the simplest things. Then he said something about messages left with Mr. Parrish's telephone service. Guess what his lawyer found out?'' She looked at Mrs. Eberhard. "Two pages of Mr. Parrish's messages were missing. Anyway, Daddy has managed to borrow the answering service book for a couple of days.''

"What's he looking for?'' Mr. Eberhard said, and the napkin that was resting on his lap slid to the floor with his movement.

"You know how sometimes when you write hard an impression shows on the page under it?''

"How very interesting,'' Mrs. Eberhard said distractedly. "Constance, you didn't like the soup?''

"Not really, Mother.''

"He's doing this himself?'' Mr. Eberhard asked. "Isn't he using someone to do the investigation part? Surely a private investigator hired by his lawyer . . .''

"Himself,'' Amanda confirmed proudly.

"Brad,'' Mrs. Eberhard reproved him. "Not everyone has the same resources.''

Amanda's cheeks burned as she went on. "The exciting thing is that Dad found a lab to do some testing on the pages in Mamaroneck, so tomorrow after work he's taking it over there.''

"Well, I certainly admire his initiative,'' Constance's mother said. "I'd let the police do it if it were me.''

"In any case,'' Mr. Eberhard said, "Amanda's a brave girl. It's not easy on a family when a respectable man finds himself in legal problems. I had a friend on Wall Street . . .''

"Please,'' Mrs. Eberhard interrupted. "Two nights ago we spent the whole evening talking about that inconsiderate girl Theresa. And now we're ruining our guest's dinner.''

"It's not the same at all,'' Constance protested. "Theresa was just a maid. But Amanda's father is a celebrity.''

"Your mother's right,'' Bradford Eberhard said. "Suppose we change the subject.'' He looked at the two girls. "Let's talk about history.''

"Okay,'' Amanda said quickly. "For ten points, give me

the most important act passed by Congress one hundred years ago.''

"The Sherman Anti-Trust Act," Constance said as her father raised his eyes to the ceiling.

"That's what they're teaching you in school?" he groaned.

Forty-one

THEY HAD EXPECTED ANY INTERCEPTION would come in front of the lab, but they were taking no chances. At exactly seven-twenty-five Flagstaff and Barzeny were waiting inside the young lawyer's new Audi 5000 at the end of Rivetz's parking lot. On Barzeny's lap was Flagstaff's Nikon with ASA 1,000 film and a telephoto lens. For his part, Leo had dummied up a book in a bright yellow manila envelope which he planned to lay conspicuously on the passenger seat next to him in his car. The idea was to photograph Eberhard making a play for the incriminating evidence, with both Flagstaff and Barzeny as witnesses. But they needed more than a photograph, which accounted, to a certain extent, for Leo's bulky profile. In his left raincoat pocket he had a tape recorder with its mike taped under his shirtfront. That was to catch the dialogue that they hoped would take away any doubt as to Eberhard's role in Parrish's death.

But Leo had no illusions as to the danger he was running in this crazy scheme, which accounted for the other lump that was in the right-hand pocket, Sollie's Smith and Wesson 29 with its four-inch barrel. It only held six shots, but Sollie had given him the warning that the .44 magnum was as powerful as a mule. "It's like a pissed-off .45," Sollie said, "with a brain. Be careful."

Flagstaff waited a full two minutes, but no one followed Leo when he pulled out of the lot. He caught up to the Dodge Valiant twelve blocks away and then dropped back a hundred yards. They knew from Leo that Eberhard had a Mercedes 560SEL which, in Westchester County, was not as scarce as a 1977 Valiant. They didn't expect that Eberhard would be careless enough to get someone else to do this little job, but there was always the chance he had gotten a different car. Also, there was no guarantee he would even go for the bait. Mamaroneck was fifteen minutes away through light traffic on local streets, which gave plenty of opportunity for other cars to weave in and out of their loose convoy. For five minutes nothing happened. They crossed over Central Avenue in Rye, then swung under Playland Parkway on their way south.

They had chosen Omega Scientific Services, housed in a small cinderblock building on the north side of town, to stage the drop-off. They liked it for two reasons: because it looked the part—the large sign in front proclaimed OMEGA SCIENTIFIC SERVICES—and also because it was located in a fairly quiet area of few businesses and fewer residences. The last thing they wanted was for Eberhard to be scared off by a lot of foot traffic.

As they traveled south it looked like they had guessed right, that any attempt on the manila envelope was going to be made in front of the laboratory. The Valiant was still one hundred yards ahead, but there were no cars in between and only an older woman in a station wagon directly behind them. A few more minutes and they'd be in Mamaroneck.

The road they were on curved left, and for a moment Leo's car went out of sight. It was at that moment that Flagstaff briefly caught a flash of light on his left.

The panel truck had come roaring across the avenue and swung in behind the Audi, just nicking the left rear fender. Both men heard the sound of metal crunching against metal and saw the station wagon that had been following them go careening onto the sidewalk and come to a stop up against a mailbox.

"Shit," Flagstaff said. "Crazy sonofabitch driver." He looked up into his rearview mirror but couldn't spot the panel truck anywhere. "Where'd he go?"

He was answered by another tap on his left rear fender from the panel truck, which was sitting off in his blind spot. Both vehicles were doing about thirty miles an hour on the open street.

"Watch out," Barzeny called, but it was too late. The truck swung out a foot to the left, then came back hard so that it pushed Flagstaff's rear into a thirty-yard fishtail. The young lawyer struggled for control of the wheel, and by the time he had it, the panel truck was back behind them.

"Is that Eberhard?" Flagstaff shouted, but Barzeny was shaking his head.

"I cannot see good inside but person driving is short, not six foot three. Head is just above steering wheel."

Flagstaff sped up from thirty to thirty-five miles an hour to put some distance between them. "Sonofabitch nailed my fender. A brand new Audi!" He stuck his head out the side window and tried to take a fast glance at his crumpled side, but that vanity cost him. Just at that moment, the vehicle behind hit the gas hard. Flagstaff glanced up in time to watch as his left tail light shattered in an explosion of glass. The panel truck pulled back again as Flagstaff faced forward and grimaced.

"What the hell's going on?" he shouted. "They're supposed to be after Leo."

"I don't think they understood message," Barzeny said as he turned and tried to get a photograph of the trailing panel truck through their rear window. "Is coming again."

This time Flagstaff mashed down on his own gas but had to let up when he saw the line of cars crossing at the red light sixty yards ahead of him. Leo's car had made it through before the light changed. He braced his shoulders for the hammer blow of the truck behind them, which came a second later. The jolt was not as unnerving as the sound of scraping and collapsing metal that came with it.

"Christ, this has got to stop. The car's not even a month old," Flagstaff said.

"Can't stop now," Barzeny shouted. "What they want you to do."

"Forty thousand dollars and an eight-month wait. Are you crazy!" He slowed down to a creep, and just as the light changed, the truck slammed into them again. The fuel-tank inlet ruptured, and the smell of high-octane unleaded seeped into the compartment where the two men were being bounced around like Ping-Pong balls.

"No more," Flagstaff shouted and pulled over to the side of the road. As the panel truck passed two shots rang out and exploded the right front tire of the Audi.

"Did you see that?" Flagstaff said, his eyes wide as fifty-cent pieces. "He shot right through his own door."

Barzeny finally managed to take a picture of the truck, now racing ahead. But neither Barzeny nor Flagstaff could imagine why anyone at Hank's Fresh Fish Market would want to run them off the road.

"Shit," Flagstaff said. "We're out of it. I have no idea how to change the goddamn tire. I never expected to get a flat with this car." He looked up at the panel truck in pursuit of the Dodge Valiant. "Leo's on his own now. Christ, this wasn't supposed to happen before the lab."

"Call Rucker," the Russian said. "Leo cannot do this alone."

"You call," the attorney said as he got out of the door and surveyed the wreck of his new car. "I've got to phone my insurance company."

Forty-two

LEO WAS UNAWARE OF THE DISAPPEAR-
ance of his backup team. The drive so far had been unevent-
ful, except that he had been so keyed up even the red lights
made him jumpy. The only thing that gave him any comfort
was the Smith and Wesson on his hip, which he felt every
now and then for reassurance.

At seven-forty-five in Mamaroneck the streetlights were
on, but many of the shop windows were closed and dark. A
light breeze was whipping papers across the road and making
the forty-three degrees feel colder than it was. When he
turned off Halstead onto Harrison he rolled the car window
up, momentarily feeling safe and protected. A patch of per-
spiration had formed at the small of his back. He knew that
in just a few minutes he would have to leave the car and
venture out into open territory. At the very least he would
have to cross ten yards where he would be an easy target if
Eberhard just wanted to shoot him and take the envelope
away.

He turned the corner on Harrison and Wilmot and slowed
the car down. Two blocks away was the building, next to a
parking lot on one side and a plumbing supply distributor on
the other. A dental laboratory across the street. The lights
were still on in the Omega Scientific Systems office, but the
street was empty of cars. Leo pulled the Valiant to the curb
and cut the motor. He swiveled in his seat to look behind
him, but in the next three minutes no other cars pulled into
the block. He was alone with one stray cat picking at a gar-

bage can on the corner and a radio beating out a salsa rhythm one or two blocks away. Leo waited. Was someone waiting in one of the cars in the parking lot? And where the hell were Flagstaff and Barzeny? They were supposed to pull in opposite him a half block away. A car passed him quickly, then a panel truck, then he was alone again with the cat and the music. Christ, what to do? The manila envelope with the dummy book was on the seat next to him, radiating evil. What the hell? He could just start the car up and take off again, forget the whole deal. But the lights were still on in the laboratory, and it was only a short walk to the building. Coming back would be a piece of cake. If Eberhard didn't pounce on the way in, it would be too late. He slid his hand into his jacket pocket and flicked on the recording unit. Then he pulled on the door handle, snatched the manila envelope, and levered himself onto the street. The steady beat of the radio was keeping perfect time with the pulse beating deep inside his neck. He closed the car door and started his walk.

Once, when he was in grade school, he had gone to buy firecrackers on a street in East Harlem. He had gone with twenty dollars in his pocket and the name of some kid who could supply him with all the ashcans and cherry bombs any thirteen-year-old could ever want. That last daunting half block flashed to his mind now. He dropped his hand to his side only inches away from the gun.

Suddenly he heard a scraping noise to his right and stopped short. It was the cat, come to investigate who this intruder was. Leo resumed walking, the manila envelope feeling like it weighed ten pounds. A few more cars came down the block, and at each one, Leo turned and watched. The cars hurried past without their drivers showing the slightest hesitation or concern for the little drama being played out on this side street. Leo swept the block ahead of him again with his eyes. The empty lot was still empty, and the Omega door now beckoned twenty steps away. He almost expected, like some horror-movie cliché, that when he finally reached his destination, Eberhard would jump out at him from behind the door. To his relief, the little lobby was empty when he entered the laboratory. A light was on in the receptionist's cubicle, but instead of a young pretty thing to greet him, there sat an older night guard reading a boxing magazine. He looked up incuriously as Leo entered.

"Lab's closed," he said.

"Sorry," Leo mumbled. "I didn't realize that." Turning to leave he spied a trash can and tossed the manila envelope in with great relief. He couldn't have felt happier if he had just defused a nuclear bomb. He stepped out into the night and ducked his head down against the wind. Goddamn, Leo thought back inside the car as he inserted his key in the ignition. What a wasted evening. Then he heard the slightest rustling of fabric from the back seat. He froze long enough for the cold muzzle of the automatic to be pressed against the base of his skull.

"Good evening, Mr. Perkins," a woman's voice said. "I believe you were expecting someone? No, don't turn around, and do me a favor," the woman said, "keep your hands on the steering wheel. I'll tell you when and where to go."

Leo reached for the steering wheel, partly because he'd been told to and partly because he needed something familiar to touch. A woman, and with a gun . . .

"Or can I call you Leo?" the voice went on. "After all, our daughters are close friends."

Leo peered into the rearview mirror and saw Pilar Eberhard's face looking back at him.

"Your husband couldn't make it," Leo managed. "So he sent you to do his dirty work? Very nice."

"Poor Bradford has no idea what's going on," Constance's mother said. "The dear lamb is so high on mergers and acquisitions he can't see the ground beneath his feet, or more likely, the noose around his neck. I'm afraid to disappoint your sexist notion that only men can be creative, but this little affair from the beginning has been a solo performance." She pushed the gun farther into the back of Leo's neck so that he winced. "That was your first mistake. The second was to think I came because of your trumped-up story about the book. I made sure to rip out two pages just so there would be no record of my call to Harmon the day he died." She brought her face closer to Leo's neck. "That's why I didn't stop you before you got inside the laboratory. However, you did give me a golden opportunity to rectify some earlier mistakes I made which I felt I couldn't pass up.''

"Mistakes?'' Leo said and realized suddenly, for whatever it was worth, that the recorder was picking up the conversation. "What mistakes? You had me fooled and Rucker has the IQ of a deer tick.''

"I was weak,'' Pilar Eberhard continued. "I let circumstances rule me rather than the other way around.'' She leaned back in the seat but still kept the gun on Leo's neck. "You see, from the beginning it was supposed to be a frame, but the wrong person walked into the picture. You, innocent and dumb.''

Leo cleared his throat and looked out the windshield. There was still no one on the block. "Instead of . . . ?''

"My husband, innocent and dumb and rich,'' she laughed, "and on the verge of being told the facts of life by one very opportunistic piano teacher. There's no getting around it, Harmon could be a son of a bitch when he wanted to. I dreamed up this sweet little thing to get out from under both of them.''

Leo's hand came off the wheel. "You were sleeping with him!'' he said with undisguised shock.

"Put your hand back. This thing has bullets in it.''

There was silence in the car for a minute after Leo's outburst.

"Yes,'' she said finally. "From Constance's third lesson. Through Bach, Mendelssohn, and Mozart.'' She laughed so explosively Leo thought the gun would go off. Just as abruptly, she stopped. "Now, we're going to drive to a very quiet spot I know, even quieter than this.''

Leo squeezed the steering wheel tighter. Driving to a quieter spot meant only one thing. His mind was racing. "Don't you think you've forgotten something?'' he finally asked. His voice shook although he had willed himself to make it as even as hers.

"I should have known,'' Pilar sneered. "Salesmen always have little tricks up their sleeves.''

"No trick,'' Leo said with hope. "Because you never

found what you were looking for in Parrish's apartment. The maid told us things weren't in their right place. So we looked. Perhaps we were more thorough.''

For a long moment she didn't speak. ''And now you're going to tell me you did, Leo. But that won't work, because nobody found it, not the police and certainly not you. If you had you would have turned it over to Rucker to save your own neck.'' She dented the back of Leo's neck with cold metal to emphasize her point. Then she relaxed. ''I did have a couple of bad hours looking for it until I realized Harmon really was exquisitely greedy. He probably sold my little impulse memento the day after he received it . . . for thousands.''

''And continued threatening to show it to your husband?''

Pilar didn't answer at first, then added, ''Or traded the watch in for cash and those appalling new cuff links I found. An engraved gold Rolex for a cheap pair of ten-karat studs.''

''No,'' Leo croaked.

''No, what?''

''The cuff links were mine.''

''How splendid. How fitting.'' Pilar laughed with true delight. Leo took the opportunity to half turn toward her.

''Parrish didn't dispose of your watch,'' he said, taking a long shot. ''He simply locked it away. And I found the safety deposit key. That sappy gift was worth more than a few thousand dollars to a man like Harmon Parrish.''

''Put both hands back on the wheel,'' Pilar said now with only a trace of merriment. ''Believe it or not, you are making my job easier, Leo. You're right, he did threaten to show it to Bradford. But I was searching for the watch not to hide it, but to make sure the police would find it. Now I can arrange for them to do just that, and when they do they'll go straight for my dear husband. They'll also finally find the other cuff link I dropped in Bradford's jewelry box, and the new G string on our piano. Rucker will figure it was Brad from the beginning, especially since he's as tall as you are. He'll figure my husband got nervous when he saw the case against you coming apart. Your wife wasn't having an affair with Harmon so there's no jealousy motive.''

"There's only one problem," Leo said. "Why would your husband be so stupid as to murder me?"

Pilar took a breath. "Who said anything about murder, Leo? There are all sorts of accidents . . ." She let that hang in the air. "And besides, I can assure you I've covered every detail. In case they do figure Bradford decided to get rid of you because you had found out about the watch, he is, unfortunately for him, without an alibi right now. He is quite alone tonight since our Irish maid left us last week," she smiled, "prompted by a healthy cash bonus from me to see her folks back in Macroom. She was getting to be a problem."

"And Constance?"

"I thought you knew," Pilar said sarcastically. "She's having another study date with Amanda tonight . . . at your house this time. Now, start the car and drive straight . . . and very slowly."

Leo leaned forward and touched his keys. As he did a little spark of an idea glimmered. He fumbled with the keys for a few moments before turning the motor on. When his hand came away it was holding his safety deposit key still attached to a one-inch ring. He transferred it to his left hand and continued talking.

"But you have another problem," he said. "You're counting on the police finding the key in my possession, or somewhere in my house. But that's not going to happen, and if you kill me, you'll never get it. You think I was foolish enough to keep Harmon's key where it could be found?" He allowed himself a smile. "I'm accused of murdering him. Makes sense that I hid it."

There was silence in the car for a moment. "You're bluffing," she said.

"Poker's not my game." He looked up in the mirror. "You mind if I open the window? It's getting stuffy in here." Without waiting, he rolled down the glass and put his left hand on the ledge. As he did so he felt the gun once again at his neck.

"But I'd be willing to make you a trade—an offer good

only tonight.'' His gallows humor amazed him. ''I give you the key, and you give me my freedom.''

''Men are so stupid, so full of themselves,'' she said unexpectedly. ''Look at you, a discount Phillip Marlowe. If you'd just let the police have that little monument to the hours the virtuoso and I had shared, then you wouldn't be in this position right now.''

''I couldn't get into the box, I tried. Besides, Rucker would say I manufactured it.''

''Maybe.'' Her eyes narrowed. ''Now start driving.'' After a moment she continued. ''I'm listening.''

Leo raced the motor before putting the car in gear, and the noise masked the sound of the falling key and ring hitting the pavement. He drew his hand back casually inside the car and pulled out slowly into the road.

''That's really all there is to it,'' Leo said. ''As far as a discount furniture salesman like me is concerned, the world won't miss one filthy-rich blue-blood capitalist named Bradford Eberhard.''

Pilar said nothing.

Leo tried again. ''Look, if it will make you feel better, I'll move my family to Florida. A guy like me doesn't have to stick around and worry a lady. You get the key, the police get the engraved watch, and I get off the hook. I hope the inscription was juicy.'' He breathed deeply. ''And maybe you'd see fit to contribute something to my relocation costs.'' What the hell, he thought, when you go fishing, the bait has to look real.

Still nothing. And then . . . ''Turn left here.''

''So, it's no deal?'' Leo asked nervously.

''Actually,'' she said pleasantly, ''it sounds like a workable arrangement.'' She thought for another moment. ''Yes, let's do that. You have the key nearby?''

Leo breathed out heavily. ''Rivetz, where I work.'' To himself he thought—two guards, plenty of light, and Sollie's old Smith and Wesson. To her he said, ''Would you care to put your gun away and join me in the front seat?''

''No thank you,'' Pilar said coldly. ''I'm used to being chauffeured.''

Forty-three

LIEUTENANT RUCKER GLANCED SIDEWAYS at the little man sitting next to him in the patrol car. I must be out of my mind, he thought, to go on a wild goose chase with some Russian derelict I've seen only once before and who, even now, speeding through the streets of Mamaroneck, sits chewing pistachio nuts. Crazy, he thought to himself, which was the same thing he had told the duty sergeant twenty minutes before on his way out of the station. And yet the little man had sounded so absolutely convincing on the telephone that against his better judgment, he had decided to humor him. He had put Barzeny on hold and placed a call to Hank's Fresh Fish Market.

"You found the stolen van already?" the owner had asked when Rucker introduced himself. Three minutes later Rucker was in a car headed for the phone booth in which the old Russian was waiting. At the very least he didn't want his chief suspect pulling stunts he knew nothing about.

"Hold on," he said and swung the Chrysler into a squealing right turn onto Harrison Avenue. He had the lights flashing and the siren on, but at this time of night the traffic had thinned out enough for him to be hitting fifty on the straight sections.

"You sure about the address?" he shouted at the old man, who simply nodded and said, "If we're not too late."

Rucker blasted through an empty intersection against the light and kept his foot on the accelerator. "Crazy," he said aloud and leaned closer into the steering wheel. "Out of my fucking mind."

The first thing they saw was the panel truck pulled to the side of a cross street a block from Omega Scientific Systems. Rucker slammed to a stop and both men got out to investigate. Except for a lingering smell of fish, the truck was empty. Barzeny pointed to the two bullet holes in the right-side door, which was enough to send Rucker back to the patrol car to call in for a backup and a lab unit for the truck. Then he started walking the short distance to the laboratory. Barzeny followed.

"I think we are too late," the older man said. "I don't see his car."

"You want to tell me again what the hell's going on here?" Rucker said, still walking. "Perkins tried to set up a trap and it backfired?"

"For Bradford Eberhard," Barzeny said. "But it was not Eberhard in truck." He moved his short legs fast to keep up with the officer. "But I think I know who it was, or who it had to be."

"Yeah, who?" Rucker said skeptically.

"His wife."

Rucker stopped and looked at the Russian in disbelief. This was good, this was real good. Apparently being pulled around on a chain by some old Bolshevik wasn't all that was on the bill for this evening's entertainment. Now he was being told that a respected CEO and his blue-blood wife had conspired to knock off a foppish piano player. Or was the mad Russian suggesting that the tiny woman alone had lifted a heavy, struggling man for as long as it had taken her to cut his blood vessels and strangle him to death? Rucker shook his head energetically, more to clear it than to tell Barzeny what he thought of his theory, and turned back toward the laboratory. In another five steps he was at the front door and trying the handle.

"She is very clever woman," Barzeny said to his back. "But I figured out how she did it."

"Not now," Rucker hissed as he gave the handle another

turn. The door was locked. He took out his service revolver and knocked on the metal frame loud enough to be heard at the far end of the building. The lights were still on, so he figured someone must still be there.

A few seconds later the door opened, and when it did they found themselves looking at one very annoyed night watchman.

"What the hell's your problem?" he started out, but shifted his tone the moment he saw the gun and the badge Rucker was flashing.

"Anyone come in this place in the last twenty minutes?" he asked.

The guard looked at him, then Barzeny.

"Nope," he said.

"You sure?" Barzeny said, frowning.

"Sure I'm sure, unless you mean that guy who walked in and right out. About fifteen minutes ago. But he didn't go back into the lab."

"That was Leo," Barzeny said to Rucker. "He was alone?"

"Far as I could tell. Could have been someone outside waiting, though. I was in there." He pointed to the telephone receptionist's desk.

"You hear any commotion or noise outside after he left?" Rucker asked.

"Nothing, but I was reading. I could've missed something."

"No shots?" Rucker persisted.

The guard's eyes opened wider.

"Hell no. Was he in some kind of trouble?"

"Did he have a yellow folder with him?" Barzeny asked over the other man's question.

The watchman hesitated, thinking. "Yup—he just threw it in the garbage. Want it?"

"Yeah," Rucker said. He gave Barzeny a look that said what he was thinking: "What a bonehead play this was." The guard handed Rucker the manila envelope.

"Thanks," Rucker said.

"Anything else?" the guard asked.

"I guess that's it." He turned and faced Barzeny. "Have any idea where your friend went . . . assuming your story isn't just a fairy tale?"

The older man shook his head slowly. "Anywhere. The woman . . . Eberhard's wife, could choose wherever." The two men walked slowly over to the road and stood for a moment. "She has gun and is not afraid to use it," Barzeny continued. "My suspicion is she waits for Leo to come out and gets him to drive somewhere." Barzeny glanced up and down the street, trying to figure a direction they might take. Then he realized it didn't matter. Within fifteen minutes they could be miles away.

The sound of a siren pierced the night. The police van screeched to a halt in front of Rucker. "Hold it," Rucker instructed Barzeny. He opened the van's passenger door and walked the police technician over to the panel truck. The van slowly followed.

Barzeny started to follow, but in the light from the street lamp he thought he caught a glimpse of something shiny in the middle of the street. He walked over, bent down with difficulty, and felt the pavement.

"Wait one moment," he called out.

"What?" Rucker yelled back.

Barzeny stood up and held a key attached to a ring in his hand. "From Leo," the old man said with a puzzled expression.

Rucker walked back and looked at the key. "Could be any safe deposit key," he said.

"Says 'Mosler,' " Barzeny said slowly. "Is his, I've seen it before."

"So?" Rucker challenged.

"Is message. He had to snap it off larger key ring to drop it."

"Sure, sure. When you figure it out, let me know," the policeman said. "Meanwhile I'll be over with the truck." He turned and walked away.

It didn't take the old Russian policeman long. In two minutes he guessed they had gone to Rivetz where Leo had left Parrish's safety deposit key.

He trotted up to Rucker. "Come," he said breathlessly. "I know where they went."

"Give me five minutes and I'll have everything squared away," Rucker said. "Maybe ten."

"Is too long to wait," Barzeny insisted. "Too late to stop trouble."

"Patience," Rucker replied. "You Russians never have any patience." He turned back to his people, and Barzeny could do nothing but curse in a language they didn't understand.

Forty-four

ON THE WAY TO THE RIVETZ WAREHOUSE Leo was having second thoughts about his plan. He would always remain a threat to her, and for someone who had murdered once, threats, like weeds, were to be eliminated.

"Can you get in without the guard?" she asked as they turned a corner and the huge building came into view.

Leo wondered if he should tell the truth. The alternative was guaranteed to buy the poor guard a one-way ticket to his local mortuary. The last thing she could afford was to be seen with Perkins.

"Yeah, I got a key," he answered. "All the inventory people out back are given one." He pointed to his key ring hanging from the ignition. "It's the long one with the blue plastic top." When he put his hand back down on the seat it brushed by the gun in his pants pocket. He gave it a thought but decided he was not ready to gamble yet. He could tell from the little vibration in his other pocket that the recorder was still running.

"Pull over there," she nodded as they entered the parking lot. "And leave the keys in the car. Just pull off the Rivetz one."

Leo parked, turned off the motor, and removed the long key.

"Now," she said, "as naturally as you can, get out of the car and walk to the door. The gun under my jacket is pointed at your spine. Anyone stops us, let me do the talking."

"My pleasure," Leo said.

They arrived at a small side door situated next to a large bay area used for loading and unloading. Leo bent down to fit the key into the lock, but before opening it he stood up.

"I think the door is wired. We go through and an alarm sounds at the guard's station."

"Good," Pilar said. "That way we won't have to bother calling him. Where does he sit?"

"Over there." Leo mentioned over to the other side of the bay area. "About forty feet."

"Go ahead and be quick."

Leo turned the key and pushed the door open. A red light started flashing over the doorframe, and a buzzer pierced the silence of the large warehouse. For a woman in her forties Pilar moved with amazing agility. She slipped quickly inside and flattened herself against a partition wall, out of view of the guard. She could still see Leo six feet away, and he could still see her and the gun leveled at his chest. They both heard the footsteps of the guard as he approached down the perimeter aisle. Leo waited, then turned slowly to face him.

"It's me, Perkins," he said. "I just came in to get something from my locker I left today."

The guard grunted something like "G'wan in," then he turned heavily to walk back to his station. Pilar whisked from behind the partition and moved quickly behind the guard. He must have figured the noise she made was Perkins's doing because he never turned around. The blow she delivered with the butt of the gun was clean and straight, and the unfortunate man dropped as though he were a puppet whose strings had been cut. Pilar turned back before Leo even had a chance to gasp. She pointed the gun at him.

"Tie him up," she said and motioned to the wall next to the loading dock where there was a reel of twine for shipping. "Consider the man lucky," she added. "All he'll have in the morning is a headache."

Leo cut off a length of rope and started wrapping the unconscious man. Never had he felt more exhausted. She had gone through his first test with ease, and from here on in there'd just be the two of them in the vast warehouse. Still, he had the gun . . .

"What's that in your pocket?" she demanded. Leo finished with the knot and turned around on his knees to face her.

"A tape recorder," he answered flatly.

"Sure, I should have known. Let's have it. Now that we made our deal," she said softly, "you won't be needing that."

Reluctantly Leo reached in, disconnected the mike wire, and removed the recorder from his pocket. The little reel was still turning.

"Slide it over." she said from six feet away.

Leo curled his toes underneath him and reached out with the little machine. Okay, Perkins, he told himself, now or never. First it's the recorder, then it's the gun, then you're finished. No way she's going to let you walk after she gets the key. Out of the corner of his eye he measured the distance to the next aisle and judged it to be about ten feet, three quick strides, time for her to get one maybe two shots off. These are going to be the most important ten feet in your life, he thought and brought his other hand closer to the pocket with the gun. She took a step closer, and in that moment, Leo coordinated his body to do four things simultaneously. He threw the recorder underhand with his left hand, he spun around completely to his right, took the first of his three strides toward the next aisle, and struggled to remove his own gun. He didn't see where the solid little recorder hit, but it must have been well aimed after years of ambidextrous softball pitching. Her shot winged off up toward the roof and shattered a fluorescent light fixture. He heard her curse and then heard the sound of the next shot and felt the bullet graze by his neck, almost as though someone had given him a little tug by the collar. He had his gun out, and as he swiveled to level a shot at her, the momentum of his two strides took his body into the next aisle. His outstretched trailing gun hand didn't quite clear the edge and crashed painfully into the steel upright. His finger jerked the trigger in reaction, sending a bullet into a replica Louis XVI gilt mirror, but the double impact made him lose his grip, and the gun clattered to the floor out in the open. He cursed to himself but was already moving down the corridor and instinctively kept going. He ran in a crazy zigzag pattern, and when he pulled up around the next corner, he was breathing hard and trembling.

Get hold of yourself, he thought, but his adrenaline wasn't cooperating. Control the breathing, he thought. The last thing he needed was to sound like The Little Engine That Could while she zeroed in on his position. Where the hell was she? He crouched down to the floor, peered around the metal partition, then bolted across the open aisle further back into the warehouse. No shot rang out and Leo hustled another thirty feet to a further aisle in the grid. Deep breath, he told himself, slow, deep breath, and he concentrated on bringing his heart rate down. Shit! He looked up and saw a cubbyhole three rows up with some room in it. Buy some time, he figured, and started upwards. It was not easy trying to climb without making noise. He passed the second-level cubby, which had a large, floral-pattern sleeper sofa in it with two matching club chairs, and kept going. Any second now he expected to see her swivel around a corner and take a shot, but nothing happened. He made the third row and slithered over the edge and under a felt-topped, oak poker table. Stacked to one side were its matching fold-up chairs, each with the same Western horseshoe motif of the table carved in their side. He lay under the poker table and listened.

He was twenty feet above the cement floor, lying on his stomach on a flat piece of sheet metal that kept him from view but was not thick enough to stop a bullet. Around him was several million dollars worth of furniture.

So, now what? he thought. Maybe he could just stay there and she'd go away. The place was cavernous, she couldn't hope to search every bin. He almost believed that until the next shot rang out. The sound came from the far wall where the warehouse funneled into the showroom. For a moment he thought she was going crazy, shooting at anything that moved in the air currents swirling through the large building. Then he heard the deep groan and realized she had aimed carefully. There were two guards at Rivetz that evening, one in the warehouse and one in the showroom. With new panic he realized how deliberate she had been in not chasing him. Leo heard a duller groan and an instant later another shot. After that, silence. Now there was no one to interfere in their deadly game. She had all night to find him. Leo looked at his watch and noted it was almost nine o'clock. Had Barzeny reached the lab? Had he spotted the key and ring? Would he figure out what it meant? He realized he was clutching at straws. There was so much light in the warehouse! Too much damn light. But leaving his cubicle in search of a master switch would be suicide. Just sit tight, he told himself. She'll get tired and go away. It would take her a week just to get the right section of the warehouse where he was. He listened carefully but didn't hear anything except the somnolent breathing of the guard she had knocked unconscious by the unloading dock. Then he thought he heard a footstep a few aisles away, closer than he expected. One hundred thousand square feet, more than two acres of floor space, and she'd already located the general area he was in! The warehouse was deathly still. Except for the clocks inside the showroom, there wasn't a moving object in the whole building. The rest of the furniture stood as testimony to the lifelessness of possessions. All those clocks, most of them mounted on the wall near the lighting department, would soon be chiming nine, the time any normal father would be at home putting his kid to sleep, not trying to avoid a murderer's bullet.

Nine o'clock. Leo briefly concentrated on that. He exposed his left wrist and saw in horror that his watch said 8:59:49. Too late! But still he struggled through the modes of operation and on/off switches, trying to remember what goddamn button it was that turned off the hourly alarm function. He had gone through half of the numbers on his watch keypad when the watch responded by sounding its loud electronic beep, signaling the start of a new hour. It also announced his exact location. A moment later he heard the scrape of footsteps. He felt like grinding his cheap watch into its component electronic chips, but moving now was out of the question. He hunkered down lower and waited.

"It was a mistake, Leo," she called suddenly. "This wasn't supposed to happen." Leo said nothing. "Sorry I had to kill the second one, he saw me. But we can still keep our little arrangement. You just give me the key, and I'll throw away my gun. You don't even have to come with me. What do you say?"

The idea was absurd. She was just playing for a response, any response to pinpoint his position in the prison of furniture. Queen's gambit declined. Her voice had come from near the juncture of aisle C and the cross aisle 4, about thirty feet away. Leo slithered an inch at a time until he could just see over the edge of the metal underneath him. On the concrete floor below, a few feet away, was a forklift truck. Over by C4 he thought he glimpsed a slight movement. He pushed back slowly and waited.

The idea of remaining cramped all night under the poker table frightened him. Maybe he'd cough, sneeze, or move and bump into something. His back was already beginning to bother him. All night was a long time. He was already uncomfortable. He twisted his head to the right and looked toward the roof. Maybe he could climb up. There were three more levels of bins on top of his, the last one open on top, then the light fixtures and the steel trusses and finally the sheet-metal roof. Not an easy climb, and he'd be exposed all of the way. And once he got there, then what? He could climb over the top bin into the next stack backing this one, but she'd have her choice of following him or simply walking around and getting him from the other side. Maybe there was no alternative to staying put. He kept hearing Barzeny's lecture about patience, but a game of chess was one thing; playing for your life was quite another.

Then he spotted the network of thin pipes suspended from the heavier network of trusses only a few feet above the top bins. An idea began to form. As new employees, they'd been told about the sprinkler system, how sophisticated it was and how, without it, the vast warehouse full of flammable objects could become a huge inferno. As Leo eyed its pipes and shower bibs, he remembered something else. If one sprinkler opened, an alarm automatically went to the local fire department pinpointing that area of the warehouse. Very sophisticated, with its electronic position-identification system, but setting one off was relatively easy. At each bib a spring control was held in check by a thin piece of special metal that melted at a low temperature. In a fire, when the temperature rose to that point, the metal melted, the springs opened, the water spurted out from the bib, and the alarm was sent. Simple, just melt the thin strip of metal with a match. Simple, that is, unless you weren't a smoker.

"I'm waiting, Leo," Pilar Eberhard called from below. "Don't make me look for you bin by bin. I know you're in this aisle."

Matches, Leo thought, where the hell are matches? In the vast warehouse, where was he going to find a small book of matches? And how was he going to search without Pilar seeing him? He remembered that with the shipment of wood-burning cast-iron replica Franklin stoves had come extra-long-necked butane lighters for reaching into the bottom of the gratings. He had seen some of the forklift jocks liberate a few as cigarette lighters. Not the kind of thing you'd stick in your pocket, so maybe if he was lucky . . . He peered over the edge carefully and this time looked more closely at the forklift truck almost beneath him. On the dashboard in front of the control levers was a copy of the *Daily News*, and just peeking out below it, the red body and trigger of a butane lighter. Leo also noted with some surprise that the keys were still in the ignition of the lift.

He looked up but this time concentrated no further than the top of the bin he was in. He needed something to divert her from the aisle, something to throw. There were only the poker table and the matching chairs, all too heavy. Then he focused on the drawer of the table and on its horseshoe-shaped brass pull. Very slowly he reached up and started turning it counterclockwise. A single center screw held the pull in place from inside. After five turns he heard the muffled sound of the inner screw falling onto the felt-lined drawer bottom, and the heavy brass pull came away in his hand. He let out his breath slowly, then very carefully raised himself up onto his elbow and hip.

"Okay, Leo," she called again. "I'm losing my patience." He heard the soft sound of rubber wheels against the smooth concrete and realized she was moving a platform ladder into place so she could inspect the stacked bins in his aisle. It would take her no more than five or six minutes to reach him.

He drew his arm back with the brass pull and made sure it wouldn't touch the table above him. He had to throw the metal accurately order into the next aisle, clearing the top of the bin facing him, and he had to do it without making any noise. It was a pitch that even Dwight Gooden might have trouble with. He made the motion once more, then brought his arm forward for real and let the metal fly. In suspended disbelief he watched as it sailed outward and upward on a trajectory that carried it soundlessly over a bin full of Formica coffee tables neatly bisecting the open space beneath the lowest roof truss. Two seconds later, he heard it bounce against the edge of a metal bin in aisle D, then clatter onto its metal floor.

Pilar didn't hesitate for a moment. She drew back from the ladder she had stationed at the beginning of aisle C and ran around the corner into aisle D. Leo gave her enough time to run halfway up that aisle before he moved. When he did, it was as though a swarm of hornets was chasing him. He swung over the edge of his bin, dropped three feet to the second row, crouched, then jumped for the seat of the forklift truck six feet lower. By some miracle, his feet landed in the right spots. He sank into the seat and turned on the ignition.

He had made enough noise in his descent to alert her to her mistake, so if the motor didn't catch, he'd be trapped. The motor ground away for two seconds that felt to him like an eternity, then kicked over. Leo shoved the truck into gear, any gear, and let the clutch out. In the same moment he grabbed the butane lighter as it bounced onto his lap.

"Son of a bitch!" he heard her shout as she ran back. But she had to dodge the ladder, and by the time she had a clear shot, he was twenty yards away and rounding a corner. The shot hit the heavy weight on the forklift's rear and ricocheted into a vinyl Barcalounger, tearing out a mushroom of fabric as it exited. Leo found a higher gear and within a few seconds had the machine up to fifteen miles an hour. Pilar ran up the length of aisle C and turned the corner, but by that time Leo had put another thirty yards between them. Still, she got off two more shots, one of which stung his ear as it whistled by. He slammed into a quick left turn and found himself cruising down aisle F, known affectionately by the salesmen as the Napoli Way. Stacked in the bins from floor to ceiling was the kind of furniture reserved for funeral parlors or cheap spaghetti joints, furniture that reached out and grabbed you by the throat and dared you to say an unkind word. Leo kept his foot on the pedal until he heard the next shot, then spun right into cross aisle 6. He was outdistancing her, but the race might end when he came to the warehouse wall. He doubted he could crash through the wall, and the forklift truck made enough noise to give her time to position herself if he doubled back. He was trapped in a deadly, real-life version of a PacMan game, but without a reset button. He shifted in his seat and looked behind him, but she wasn't visible, and what was worse, he couldn't hear her running anymore. He kept going straight, passing aisles H, I, and J. There were six more letters left, but before that, he turned the forklift truck right again on K and headed for the warehouse front. He came out on the other side of the loading dock and braked in front of the large electrical panel controlling the overhead lights. Thank God he had remembered correctly. In seconds he threw every electrical switch he could hit and removed the four big cartridge fuses. All the powerful overhead lights went off except for the ever-present emergency exit lights, which cast the vast warehouse into pockets of eerie shadows. He was just climbing back on the truck when she suddenly appeared three aisles away in her stocking feet. He hadn't heard her because somewhere she'd kicked off her shoes. The bullet she fired shattered on the forklift housing, and a piece of the projectile imbedded itself into his right shoulder. He winced as he stepped on the gas and spun into aisle L. Before he abandoned the lift truck, he had one last thing to do.

Driving unsteadily, he played around with the levers until he found the one that made the fork go up. He brought the two steel prongs to eye level, then headed for the end of the warehouse. In the dim light he could just see where a sprinkler bib was positioned at the end of aisle P and halted the truck underneath it. Then he placed the *Daily News* on one of the flat forks in front of him and lit the paper's edge with the butane lighter. As it started to burn, he pulled back on the up lever. By the time the fork passed the thirty-foot level, the flame was fanning up an additional three feet. He extended the fork as high as it would go, which was about four feet shy of the sprinkler system. Then he played with the other lever, tilting the fork back and forth until the burning paper was directly under the bib. He jumped down and ran up aisle P until it intersected with the main center crossing. There, in the corner bin, he found a heavy Mission-style sideboard and hid behind it. The whole operation had taken no more than twenty seconds. But why the hell hadn't the bib gone off? He waited but nothing happened. The burning paper was too far below the bib. Damn! Then he saw some movement at the other end of the aisle and watched as Pilar mounted the truck. She had figured it out in an instant, and without putting down the two guns she was now holding, she jockeyed with the levers. The fork started lowering slowly and with it the burning newspaper. Leo bit his tongue to stop the curses from rolling off it.

But the sprinkler metal must have been partially melted because three seconds later Leo heard a crack as the spring tore open the valve. A gush of water rained down on the far end of the aisle. With it, an alarm went off somewhere up front. The electronic control system was even more sophisticated than Leo had figured because instantly the five surrounding shower bibs also released, sending a monsoon into aisle P. Pilar was instantly drenched, but it had little effect on her intentions. She realized Leo must be close and was now inspecting the bottom bins, one by one. In the dim light it was taking her some time, but she was steadily making her way toward his hiding place. How long would the fire department take to arrive? Ten minutes? Fifteen? She'd reach him first. The sideboard was a poor shield, especially since she could see his legs underneath it. Leo quickly looked around the adjoining bins for a better hiding place. Dining tables and chairs everywhere, flimsy pieces of wood and glass that wouldn't stop a bullet shot from an air rifle. Then he spotted it and hesitated only for as long as it took for him to remove his shoes. Slowly he edged out from behind the sideboard and waited until Pilar was inside one of the bins. Then he silently ran across the intersection of the two aisles and ducked behind Orantes's folly, the two-thousand-pound marble dining room table. At least it would stop a bullet, he thought. He crouched down behind the heavy table leg and caught his breath. The alarm was still sounding somewhere off to the right, but Pilar wasn't letting it affect her. She'd find him, shoot him down, and flee. The odds were on her side no matter how wet and noisy this deadly game had become. All Leo could do was wait and hope he'd figured the odds wrong. And still she came, bin by bin. Three minutes later she was searching the bin with the Mission sideboard across the way. Leo was frantic. Where the hell was the fire department? He was just getting ready to make another silent dash when he saw her look down at the tracks his feet had left in the wet cement floor as he had moved positions. Too late! Pilar had turned and was now following the tracks as they lead into aisle O and the marble table. Slowly, deliberately, she advanced until she was standing no more than five feet away. She had both guns extended and said softly to him, "Okay, Leo, game's over. Stand up."

All Leo could think of was how stupid he had been to begin with, and over what? A lifeless possession, a pair of cuff links, an obsession as insane as the table he was crouched behind. He uncurled and stood up. Slowly, he raised his hands over his head.

"Forgive me, Leo," she said almost tenderly. She pushed the gun forward a few inches. "I don't have the time or luxury anymore to get the key. I'll have to take my chances on Rucker finding it. It really is over."

"No, is not, not quite," they both heard. Leo turned to the left and saw a familiar face. The old Russian policeman was walking down the center aisle. Barzeny's eyes were set in a hard stare and he stopped thirty yards away. "Not quite," he repeated. "Now here is another to kill. You see, never does it end, Mrs. Eberhard. Like the killings Comrade Stalin ordered in the thirties. First one, then another, then the whole government." He shifted his weight from one leg to another. "What will you do about Lieutenant Rucker?" he continued. "Who is also on way but is delayed in details about stolen van? You were lucky with him from beginning. In Russia he would be janitor." He took another step closer. "But I got impatient. Sorry Leo, most times patience is best, but once in a while, not."

"You are a foolish old man," Pilar snarled. "One more dead man doesn't matter to me." She left one gun trained on Leo's chest and swung the other in the direction of Barzeny.

"My path is bleak," Barzeny said with an odd lilt, "Before me stretch my morrows, A tossing sea, foreboding toil and sorrows. And yet I do not wish to die, be sure: I want to live—think, suffer, and endure." He smiled at her. "Pushkin. Forgive please this foolish old man." He sighed. "As old investigator, I like theories confirmed. You killed Parrish with . . . how you sailors say . . . main sheet?"

A new look came across Pilar's face, a look of pleasant surprise. There she was, pointing loaded pistols at two men and looking for all the world like the winner of a fifth-grade spelling bee.

"Yes," she said. "Good guess."

"Not guess," Barzeny replied. "Had to be something like that, looking at evidence, especially clean fingernails of Parrish. Murderer did not get close to him. You must have worked hard, hard labor after killing him.''

"Too hard," she said. "He wasn't worth all the effort."

Leo raised his hands a few inches higher, wincing with the pain from his wounded shoulder. "What are you two saying? I'd like to be let in on the secret before the curtain.''

Pilar looked as if she was about to say something when a long, distant siren surprised her. It was followed by a closer, shorter squeal.

"I'm afraid I don't have the time," she said smoothly and just as gracefully pulled the trigger of the gun in her right hand. The bullet caught Barzeny in the right leg, and he sank down beside a bookcase with a tag on it that said CLEARANCE SALE. He tried to drag himself the few feet further to safety. She pulled the same trigger again, but the bullet skipped on the cement floor behind him. Maybe she didn't realize she'd missed because she immediately turned her attention on Leo. She never noticed the low noise the marble cylinders made in the bin above her as they rolled down the slight incline. Before she pulled the trigger again, one heavy marble lamp knocked the gun from her hand and pushed her onto the tabletop. Her cry of pain lasted only as long as it took for the second marble lamp to drop, crushing her neck into the polished tabletop. Leo heard two distinct cracks, one louder than the other. He watched in horrified fascination as the heavy dining room table split in the middle, and the two pieces angled inward toward each other, squeezing Pilar's lifeless body between them. The first crack had been the sound of her spinal cord snapping. Now her form lay wedged between the two angled slabs. A gun was still in her right hand and her eyes were frozen in final surprise. Only the water spraying from the overhead sprinkler disturbed the silence of death.

When the firemen rushed in three minutes later, the water on the cement floor where she had died was tinted pink. By the time Rucker arrived ten minutes after that, the water had been shut off, Barzeny and Perkins had been ambulanced to a nearby hospital, and the firemen had lifted the heavy stone from Pilar's body. The lieutenant was left to make sense of two corpses, an unconscious guard, two guns, a flooded warehouse, a ton of smashed marble, and an irate fire marshal. When the marshal had vented his venom over his men doing police department work, he remembered to hand Rucker the tape recorder Perkins had asked him to retrieve before he fainted.

Forty-five

LEO PUSHED HIS ROOK TO A6 AND SAT back with a grin. He had just successfully pinned Barzeny's queen. Both men wore hospital gowns and robes, and both sat somewhat uncomfortably over the chessboard in the visiting lounge. Barzeny had his right leg in a bandage with a set of crutches positioned nearby, while Leo had his shoulder swaddled and his arm in a sling. The fact that they remained guests of the Westchester County Hospital had less to do with their wounds and more to do with Rucker's desire to keep them somewhere he could find them. Barbara had come by as soon as she heard Leo had been injured, and on the next morning she brought along Amanda and newspapers. The chess set made an appearance on her third visit.

The newspapers had garbled versions of what had happened at the Rivetz warehouse from their police sources, but the stories all implicated Pilar in homicide.

The ordeal for Leo and his family was soon to be over. But now it was four in the afternoon, the two men were alone, and Leo had Barzeny on the defensive.

"Your move," Leo said. "And while you're thinking, perhaps you could finally get around to telling me how a

woman easily eight inches shorter than Parrish could lift him
up and kill him? Even if she stood on a chair, she was so
little he could have easily fought her off." He raised his eyes
up to Barzeny's face. "She did it with a sheet, one of the
missing ones from the bed?"

Barzeny laughed and shook his head. "I must play chess
and at same time explain murder? You do not make things
easy, Leo." He looked down at the board for a moment,
then leaned back. "No, not bed sheet, a main sheet."

Leo looked puzzled.

"The rope from boom to sailboat. That, and block and
tackle attached to it. Whole thing is removable. She set hers
up from light hook over Parrish's bed. She comes into apartment while Parrish sleeps and quietly connects all. This explains why we see broom in bedroom, to lift apparatus up to
hook.

"How I know this? Blanka Sologyar tells me Parrish never
cleans, not even for simple sweep."

Barzeny took a breath. "So, next Eberhard woman makes
small loop in end that normally goes to sail and quickly brings
it down a few inches above Parrish's head, careful not to
wake him. Then in two, three seconds she slips the garrote
around neck and puts two handles through the loop. All is
complete. He wakes, but before he knows what is happened,
she pulls down on free end and up music man goes, dragged
by wire garrote. With good block and tackle from sailboat
she could lift two hundred pounds easy this way. Also this
explains ambidextrous thing of which Ingrahm is so proud.
Not ambidextrous, just one weight pulling evenly on sides of
wire.

"Remember, Leo, your daughter telling of problems they
had using boom only a few days after murder . . . something
about tangled lines? Must have gotten it wrong when she put
contraption back. Amanda's comment started me thinking,
along with problem of the fresh sheets."

"The bed sheets now," Leo said, trying hard to follow.

"Yes, bed sheets. The body had to be found in other part
of apartment away from ceiling hook, and this means she
had to clean away that trail of blood. But Eberhard woman

is up to any challenge. While she had him swinging in air, it is easy to secure end of rope, tape a few clean garbage bags around body, let him down away from bloodstained bed, then drag him into hall. Only then she removes bags and it looks like he was killed where she places him and where blood was now collecting. But she has to get rid of blood on the bed.''

"Which meant clean sheets," Leo supplied, "and getting rid of the blanket and mattress cover.''

"Exactly. She stuffs everything into bloody garbage bags and takes everything when she goes. First she searches for her gift to him . . . you said it was a watch?''

Leo nodded.

"She wants it to be there. But she never sees key. Many hours she is there with body, looking.'' He narrowed his eyes. "Very cold-blooded.'' Barzeny leaned forward and moved a chess piece. "Maybe it works if not for you.''

"Or you," Leo added and looked down at the board. "What's that?'' he asked, frowning.

"Check," Barzeny said with a muffled grin. "Sometimes we use queen as decoy.''

Leo winced in frustration.

"But is most dangerous. Most times,'' the old chess player expanded, "innocents blunder using this strategy and never recover. Only the masters know when to use decoys.'' He patted his bandaged leg. "When there is no alternative.''

Leo looked up into the other man's smiling eyes. "You didn't have to put yourself in such danger,'' he said.

"What, and lose a good chess opponent? Besides, you forget, my people invented Russian roulette.''

The two men were silent for a moment as they studied the board. After a moment, Barzeny spoke again.

"Who was man that came earlier, Leo, one who said 'feel better' but didn't mean it?''

"Orantes.'' Leo chuckled. "Son of a bitch started off by telling me how sorry he was for all my troubles and ended by totaling exactly how much damage I'd caused.''

"So you are fired?'' Barzeny asked.

Leo shook his head. "No, the Rivetz management couldn't

do that now with all the publicity. Orantes ranted about his table and then surprised me with an offer he said had come from upstairs, although I'm sure he had a lot to do with it. He assured me I could take over a department in the Rivetz location in Tampa, Florida. Sort of what I've always wanted.''

''And you are going?'' Barzeny asked.

Leo looked at the nearby newspaper with its sixty-point headline declaring SHOOTOUT AT DISCOUNT FURNITURE OUTLET, then shifted in his seat. ''I told him,'' Leo said slowly, ''that I wanted my old job back selling dining room tables. Barbara and Amanda and I have had enough disruption in our lives.''

A little smile started forming at the corners of the old Russian's face.

''And also,'' Leo reddened, ''I hated the idea of losing such a great chess partner.'' He touched Barzeny's arm. ''I mean teacher—and friend.''

''In this case,'' his opponent said, ''I think now you will find it is mate in two.'' He offered his hand. ''So, how about another game?''

About the Author

Richard Barth is a goldsmith and an assistant professor at the Fashion Institute of Technology. He lives in Manhattan with his wife and two children.